1

It feels like my stomach is slowly crawling up my throat, threatening to eject itself onto the tops of my shoes as I sit on the overcrowded bus on the way to my new school, two thousand miles away from home. I've been in this small North Carolina town for a little over a week and I'm still not used to seeing so much green, not in contrast to the usual reds and browns of Arizona. The side of my thumb goes to its natural place—between my two front teeth, as I gnaw on the pink skin. I have a seat to myself this early in the morning, and I'm hoping that my bag next to me in the seat will help me keep the seat to myself for the rest of the ride. Mom says I'm a bit antisocial, but that's not true, I don't think. I'm social around people I feel comfortable around, not that I've felt comfortable around anyone in the past few years. Before I knew there was something different about me, I had a few close friends. Since they found out what makes me different, however, I've been shunned from the group. Luckily, if I can even call it that, my dad moved us across the country, and the times I'd spent with my friends are just memories, but not the kind I can revisit on social media since my former friends blocked me.

For months leading up to the move, I'd had to keep my secret from my parents and beg my old friends to keep it to themselves. I'd thought they could be trusted, regardless of the way we'd all been raised in our conservative church, but as soon as they found out, they acted like we hadn't all been friends since we were toddlers in our church daycare. After their initial reactions where they accused me of trying to touch them at sleepovers or secretly thinking about them in ways I'd never thought of them, I'd tried to cover my tracks—to tell them I was joking or that I had made a mistake, but it was too late. They'd made up their minds about me, and there was no taking it back. They'd only agreed to keep my secret between our group when they learned my family was leaving. Once it was confirmed that I was leaving, they cut me off, erasing my existence in the group completely, not just online.

My parents never asked what happened between me and my friends in the weeks leading up to our move, not that they noticed the shift in me. My parents have never really cared about what was going on in my life. As far as they're concerned, as long as I'm keeping my grades up and going to church every Sunday, the rest of my life isn't that important. I think most kids would love to be accepted by their families—to have the kind of family dynamic where the parents and the kids are best friends, but my parents don't believe in that dynamic. In fact, they're totally against it. My parents and I don't really talk at all. Truthfully, they barely talk to each other. We all have our roles in the house: my dad being the patriarchal breadwinner, my mom being the servant to my dad, and me being the obedient child who doesn't seem to exist unless I've done something they don't approve of. It shouldn't be a surprise to anyone that my parents don't know anything about me—not that I'd ever let them.

After getting off the loud, overcrowded bus, all without having to share my seat—advantage of being the new kid, I grab my schedule from the front office. I'd been one of the few upperclassmen on the bus, which is a bit embarrassing. Some guy had asked me if I was a freshman, probably because I looked as nervous as the freshman did, and all I could think to do was slink away from him and gnaw harder on my thumb, hoping he would leave me alone. He did, finally, when some other guy got his attention. As I sat on the cracked leather seat that somehow smelled of gasoline, my knees tucked up between my body and the seat in front of me, I'd wished I could get this day over with already and go back to my room, which still isn't completely unpacked.

    The woman behind the front desk, in the kind of blouse my mom buys from the clearance rack, welcomes me to Martin Luther King High School. She seems nice enough with her permanently orange tanned skin and gaudy eyeshadow up to her plucked-too-thin eyebrows. She has a smile like my mom's, I notice like her mouth is smiling, but there's nothing behind her eyes. I glance over the schedule she's given me after thanking her. I chose the hardest classes as an excuse to stay up in my room for the next two years, but I swear I'm not antisocial. There are things in this life that I want, and none of those things include following my parents' footsteps. I want to be somewhere cool, like a city I can be myself in. Maybe somewhere like California, or anywhere near the ocean, since I've made it my life's mission to save the sea turtles, a dream I've had since I was little and I saw a video with a piece of straw stuck inside of a turtle's nose.

    The main hallway, like the bus, is overcrowded and the conversations blend together into a loud wave broken up with short bursts of laughter—the shrillness making me uneasy. My eyes scan passively over all the new faces, most of which don't seem to notice me from the wall next to me. Each of the faces that pass is unfamiliar and my stomach hurts when I think of meeting new people. Each time someone looks at me, probably not even looking at me, my blood goes cold with fear. I wonder if my secret is written on my skin. I cautiously touch my face, in case I had somehow written it there. Looking back at my hands, I swear there's red ink transfer, but then I blink and it's gone. My secret is kept safe from all of them trapped in my chest where I should have kept it but is now locked back up tighter than ever.

    I round a corner as I squeeze through a group of students standing in a packed circle in the middle of the hallway, much to the dismay of everyone else around them. An elbow connects with my upper arm, but I ignore it. After I find my locker, my hands shaking as I twist the dial and grab what I need, I head back down the hallway. I'm looking back down at my schedule searching for the room number when my shoulder connects with someone's arm.

"Watch it." The girl's voice is low and there's aggression behind it.

I look up and in front of me next to some lockers is the most beautiful girl I've ever seen. She's tall with shoulder length straight black hair that looks a little green beneath the lights, and hazel eyes. She has a black ring sitting in the middle of her bottom lip and is dressed head to toe in black, including combat boots and a black denim vest. The vest and pants are both covered in patches—varying bands and causes she must care about. I'm both intrigued by her and terrified of her.

For a moment, I'm frozen. She has warm brown skin, high cheekbones, full lips, a wide nose, and a strong masculine jawline. Her eyes are intense and her thick eyebrows seem to be naturally squeezed together. I blink, flicking my tongue against my bottom lip, nervously. "I'm sorry," I stammer. I hold up my schedule. "I was just looking for my first class."

Her eyes scan me before she leans her shoulders back against the lockers, holding her notebook by her hip. "Who did you piss off to be dropped at this shit hole?" I don't say anything, unsure if she's actually asking me. "You are new, right?"

I hold my binder to my chest. "Yeah," I try to sound casual, but I can hear my voice shake, and I clear my throat.

She takes the paper from my hand and looks over it. I bounce on the balls of my feet, forcing myself not to look at her. She side-eyes me, then hands me the schedule back. "Come on, weirdo," she gestures with her chin. "We have the same first period."

I fold the schedule and put it in the pocket of my binder. "I'm Casey, by the way."

"Yeah, I read that," she says as she walks by me. She glances back at me. "I'm Nova."

The classroom is nearly full of students who seem to be talking all at once, yelling across the room, and dropping cuss words like they words are confetti. There's paper being thrown across seats and the tapping of nails on cell phone screens. I notice that the teacher's desk sits empty, and I'm not sure if I should sit or stand by the desk and wait. At my old school, the teacher would introduce the new student, then have them tell the other students an interesting fact about themselves. I think about what would happen if I told my secret, broadcasted it proudly to strangers, but then I consider the consequences and decide that if I were to say a fact about myself, it would be that I love jellyfish.

"Over here." Nova's voice permeates through the others and I see that she's already sat down.

There's an empty seat next to hers in the back of the classroom and she's gesturing for me to sit in it. I guess I shouldn't wait for the teacher, then. I slide between the rows, accidentally interrupting conversations, which is met with disgusted looks, and sit in the seat next to Nova. She puts her legs up over the top of the desk and crosses her ankles, her boots looking gigantic. I sit normally, one hand in my lap with the other by my mouth, as my eyes take in my new surroundings.

"You're not going to have any skin left on that thumb if you keep chewing on it," Nova says, watching me. She's not teasing me, not like my friends used to do at my old school. She's stating a fact with the slightest grin on her lips.

I interlock my fingers in my lap. "Yeah, I guess."

She crosses her arms, her attention going elsewhere. "High school is the same anywhere you go. There's a hierarchy of jocks who get away with date rape every Friday night, but they never get in any trouble for it because their families are rich and white." Her eyes go across me again. "No offense."

"No worries," I shrug.

"There's also the nerds who spend their allowances on shiny cardboard, the anime kids who think they're going to find women who actually look like that, and so on." Her eyes go to one of the guys all clad in camouflage like he's in the woods and not in the white halls of a school. "Any of those where you're from?"

"I think those are everywhere," I grin. I look around the room some more. "It's nice to see girls here who don't all dress the same." Back at my old school, we all dressed alike, mostly due to the conservative ideals my small community held.

Nova smiles, her lip ring resting between her two front teeth. She's pretty when she smiles, the way her eyes crinkle at the edges. "Have an eye for girls, then?"

"What?" I feel the panic rising in my chest and there's a scenario playing in my head that has me feeling lightheaded, thinking I've been outed—again.

"I'm joking," she says, smiling. "I do that sometimes."

I exhale, allowing my brain to slow down a little. "Oh." I fake a laugh. "You're funny."

"My friends think so," she laughs.

By lunch, I've got most of the school layout memorized. Nova helped a little, but after our first class, the friends she had mentioned talked with her in the hallway, and I didn't want to bother them. The school itself may not be that different from my old one, but the atmosphere definitely is. Even though I live in a nice house, this school, the only public school in my district, is a little rough. My parents would use certain words to describe the school that I'm not comfortable even thinking, and my old friends would probably laugh as to where I've ended up, but the school isn't so bad. There have been a couple of almost fights in the halls already, one of which I was nearly dragged into when I accidentally looked at one of the girls involved longer than she must have liked, but nothing serious.

There's a nice public school a few miles away, but since we don't live in that district ever since the schools rezoned after we'd bought the house, I couldn't get in. My parents wanted me in the private Christian school, Brunswick Christian, which includes uniforms and daily morning services in the on-campus church, but the idea of going there was worse than anything that could happen at this school. I'd take a black eye over a pleated skirt any day. To prevent having to go to the private Christian school, I purposefully mailed in the papers late and 'forgot' the admission fee in the envelope, which my mom had purposefully written a check for. My parents weren't happy that I had dropped the ball on that school, but there was nothing they could do. I don't know what's going to happen next year, but I don't want to think about that.

I catch up to Nova in the lunch line and then follow her outside to the tables. There are tables positioned under an awning to the right of the cracked sidewalk while others are scattered out on the grass that desperately needs water. There's a wire fence that surrounds the courtyard, enclosing us in with some twisted wire up toward the top, close to barbed wire, but less prison-like.

"What's with the fence?" I ask as we walk through the courtyard.

She looks to the fence and scowls. "They've got to keep the cattle herded somehow."

Her comment makes me laugh, but when she looks at me, I realize she's serious. The fence stands about ten feet tall and I can see where there are places bent from climbing attempts. The courtyard has broken concrete in places and tables with a little rust around the hinges beneath the green plastic coverings, which have weathered. The table Nova takes me to is the closest table to the fence. It sits half on the concrete and half on the grass. It's warm outside and the thin clouds keep going in front of the sun, casting shadows across everything.

At the table, I recognize Nova's friends from the hallway earlier. On the left side on the bench seat is a guy sitting with his back to the fence, a cigarette hanging out of his mouth. His skin is dark and his eyes are matching. He's dyed his hair blonde, the yellowness a stark contrast to his skin. The girl next to him on the bench seat is Japanese, I think, and she has silver rings on either side of her bottom lip. She's braiding a piece of her pastel pink hair that has fallen over her shoulder. On the right side of the table, not on the bench, is a guy who has light olive skin and has shaved his head nearly bald. Upon further inspection, I notice his wheelchair. His eyes are a sharp blue and he has a black ring in his nostril. He's typing something on an old laptop in front of him.

Nova sits her tray down on the table and I join her, carefully sliding into the bench next to her without connecting my knees against anyone on the other side of the table. As soon as I'm settled, I notice the eyes that scan me, making me feel like a goldfish in a fishbowl. I'm waiting on one of them to tap the glass just because they can.

Nova juts her thumb to me, casually, while she eats with the other. "Guys, this is Casey. She just moved here."

They each give Nova their own confused look. The girl with pink hair flings her braid back over her shoulder. Her caramel colored eyes take in my face. "Kaida," she says, introducing herself. I notice her teeth are crooked. "My pronouns are she/her."

I've read about pronouns online before, but I've never heard someone clarify their pronouns out loud. "I'm also she/her," I tell them, hoping I said it correctly.

"As am I," Nova tells me. "Just to clarify."

The guy at the laptop looks over the screen momentarily, looking at me. "Lars. He/him." He seems disinterested in what's going on and his eyes flick back down to the laptop in front of him.

The guy across from me takes a drag off of his cigarette. He must not care that smoking at school isn't allowed. "J.J. They/them," they say, exhaling smoke. They eye me, seemingly annoyed that I'm here. "Nova, where did you find her?"

I look at each of them and realize they're all dressed similarly. The only color between them is Kaida's hair and neon pink leather skirt, which she has over black fishnet stockings with boots that look similar to Nova's. I look down at my own clothes, realizing how different I look to the rest of them: a white blouse with ruffles at the chest with pinhole details, plain light blue jeans, beige flats, and straw blonde hair that I have tied half up. I definitely stick out in this group, which is the opposite of what I'm used to.

"Neverland," Nova says sarcastically. "Where do you think, dumbass? The hallway."

J.J flicks the ash off of their cigarette, their eyes flicking over to me. "What do you know about systematic racism?"

Their question catches me off guard. "Um..." I don't know how to answer them. If I say the wrong thing, they could think I'm uninformed, or worse, racist. I try my shot anyway, thinking about an article I read online over the summer. "I think I read somewhere that the prison system is modern-day slavery since drugs are pumped into impoverished areas which causes people of color to be dealers out of desperation, and therefore thrown in prison for life."

All the eyes in the group go to me and for a second, I think I've said the wrong thing and I'm preparing myself to be ostracized from the group, forced to find other people to hang out with. J.J puts their fist out for me to bump. I do, a bit awkwardly.

They take a drag from their cigarette. "Nice one," they say to Nova about me. Nova glances at me with an impressed look on her face.

Kaida looks at me like she's trying to figure me out, gnawing on her chapped bottom lip. "So, Casey, what's your deal?"

"My deal?" I've barely touched the food on my plate, so I pick up a fry and hold it between my fingers.

She nods, "Yeah, like, where are you from? Why'd you move here? You know, your deal."

Nova looks at me out of the corner of her eye, waiting for me to answer. Maybe she's just as curious about me as I am about her. I pop the fry in my mouth. "Arizona. My dad's finance company moved him out here to a new branch or something." I smooth down my blouse, looking for any excuse to get the attention off of me, which is hard when I'm the new person in the group.

Kaida sips the soda in front of her. "So, that's why you dress like that, your parents have money."

She doesn't phrase it as a question, but I take it as one. I glance down. "What's wrong with my clothes?"

Nova glares at Kaida. Kaida doesn't take the hint. "Nothing. You just remind me of Jesus camp kids."

I know she doesn't mean it as an insult, but that doesn't make it hurt any less. My hand goes to the collar of my blouse, which sits at the bottom of my throat. "I was never much into the idea of camp."

J.J puts out their cigarette on the concrete next to their boot. "Are you a Jesus freak?"

They all look at me, except for Lars, who still has his nose in his computer and doesn't seem to be involved with anything else going on in the world.

The truth is, I haven't been religious for a long time, for my own reasons. "No," I tell the group.

"How come? You seem the type," J.J asks, popping a mint into their mouth.

I think for a few seconds, trying to come up with a good excuse that doesn't out me. "Come on, guys. Enough with the third degree," Nova says. Her eyes flick to me. "Sorry."

J.J looks at me and for a second, I think they can read my mind. I try not to smile too much at Nova, or even look at her too long. My old friends accused me of doing the same, so now I'm careful about who I look at, and for how long. I don't know if J.J's face always looks skeptical or if it's just for me, but I look down at my plate anyway.

"We're just trying to get to know her," J.J says.

"We're all going out tonight," Kaida says and I realize she's talking to me, maybe changing the subject, so I look up from my plate. "There's this show downtown. You in?"

I look to Nova who nods. "You should come," she says. "It's a good way to meet like-minded people."

My stomach does a flip. She knows. She knows my secret and that I'm attracted to her. She's going to out me to everyone. When she says like-minded, she means people who are LGBT. Does that mean she's gay too? Is J.J? Kaida? Even Lars? My mind is spinning and I can feel my heart rate climb.

"Like-minded people?" The words stammer out of my mouth and I can hear how nervous I sound.

Nova shrugs absentmindedly. "Yeah, you know, activists. People who give a shit about what's going on in the world."

"Right," I sigh. I feel my heart rate slow to normal and my brain stops spinning at a million miles an hour. She doesn't know, I tell myself. No one does.

Nova's waiting on my answer. "So, what do you think?"

The truth is, I'd love to go to the show with Nova. I want to see inside her world, to see what exactly it is that she does, despite my nervousness. She says she and her friends are activists, but I haven't figured out what for, aside from her patches. I don't know Nova well or her friends that well, but Nova is really nice. Unfortunately, my parents wouldn't think great things about her. My parents think people who wear all black and go against the government are against God. They'd never let me be around Nova or any of them.

"I have a curfew," I say. "I'm not allowed to go anywhere after school."

Though is it true that I have a curfew, it's not necessarily true that I'm not allowed to go anywhere after school. I just know that if my parents found out I was out with atheist punk activists, they'd ground me for the rest of my life. Plus, my family might be what others consider racist. They're not actively burning crosses or anything like that, but they're definitely the type to lock the doors in the car when someone black or brown walks by.

J.J and Kaida exchange a look. I know that look well. It's the kind of look that people give each other when they're around someone they don't like. It's the kind of look that makes me think I have a sticker on my forehead that says 'lame'. My old friends would have that same look on their faces when I'd decline an offer to go to a party in the desert. I know I'm not as cool as Nova and her friends, and they know it too. I bet Nova probably regrets being nice to me this morning, and I don't blame her. I'm boring in every sense of the word. My old friends would tell me so to my face, not caring if they hurt my feelings.

Nova is in my next class sat in what seems to be her usual place, at the back of the class. Her legs are once again propped up on the table and her arms are crossed across her chest. I think she hates school. I think she's one of those kids, like me, who finds school boring because it's not hard enough. From what I've seen so far, Nova is really smart, but she doesn't show it off. She's the type to silently surpass the kids at the top. She has earbuds stuck in her ears as if she's trying to tune out the world or make the rest of the world think she doesn't want to participate. Her eyes land on me and she motions her chin to the seat next to hers.

I feel her watching me as I dig a pencil from my binder, but as soon as I look at her, she turns her head away, like she didn't mean to be caught. The teacher scolds Nova for having her feet up and her earbuds in. Nova does as she's told, but makes a little bit of a show of taking her feet off the desk before she sits lounged back, arms still crossed over her chest. The teacher continues with the lesson, which I'm not even paying attention to because all I can think of is Nova and how lunch ended with a tinge of awkwardness between her and her friends when she defended me. I glance over and try to think of something to say, but the words escape me. All I can do is bite my thumb and stare ahead, my eyes unfocused as I dive into my thoughts.

When the bell rings, I linger in my seat as I put my things away. Nova stands next to my desk holding her notebook. She lays a torn bit of paper on my desk, taps the paper for emphasis, and a grin, then walks out of the classroom. When I open the folded piece of paper, there's a number written on it in lime green gel pen. Nova's name is written in beautiful cursive underneath, and then a simple 'text me' with an x near the bottom.

I enter Nova's number into my phone once I'm on the bus, this time forced to sit next to a freshman girl with headphones in. Maybe it's stupid, but the way Nova wrote her name is really romantic and there's something special about knowing that green is her favorite color, which I'm basing on her pen color choice. As I sit on the bus waiting to get to my stop, I try to think of something cool to say as my first text to her. I decide on something that not many people know.

 Casey: Octopuses have three hearts

♀

 Mom is sitting at the dining table with her eyes on her laptop. She's had her own business making Christian prints for the past few years since she quit her daycare job. She designs prints with scripture written on them in some trendy way and people put them on their walls, their cars, and anywhere else they want. She's in a few specialty boutiques back in Arizona, but most of her business is online, so she mostly works from home. I think she's trying to get some business here, but she's only mentioned it once or twice.

 "Come look at this," she says from behind her laptop. From where I am at the base of the stairs, she can see me from her chair in the dining room. I lean over her shoulder at the laptop. "Joyce asked me to make some vinyl for the WBSG." (Women's Bible Study Group). There's a brag in her voice that I don't mention.

 Last Sunday was our first time at the local church my parents scouted out when we learned we were moving out here. Mom managed to become friends with a few of the women on social media after she found their names on an online church bulletin. Mom had obviously told them everything about her work at our church in Arizona because we were welcomed with open arms.

 There's a graphic on the screen that's bright teal with a gold cross in the middle. White text is underneath the cross. It's Philippians 4:13 "I can do all things through Christ who strengthens me," I read. "It looks really nice, Mom."

 She nods once, approving my approval. She slides her glasses back over her eyes and adjusts the laptop screen. "Joyce's nephew goes to your school. Did you meet Patrick today?"

I think back and I don't remember hearing the name. "Is he a junior?"

She stays looking at the screen, looking over her work. "Sophomore, but Joyce says he's mature for his age."

I keep my eye roll behind her head. "Yeah, okay," I say passively. "I'll be upstairs." She waves me away.

As I sit upstairs at my desk, the same one from my old room that has a chip in the paint from the moving truck, I run my hand over the wood beneath the desk. There are rough engravings I'd made with my old friends. We'd taken our pencils and etched our initials into the bottom with plus signs to indicate that we'd be friends forever. We'd also taken some markers and drawn pink and orange flowers to make it pretty, but kept it a secret from my parents who don't encourage ruining furniture. I think back to before I was outed and how they'd make comments about the girls at school who were out, the girls I was jealous of. I'd admire those girls' quick kisses and quiet conversations.

Those thoughts are pushed out of my head and my hand comes back from beneath the desk when my phone goes off. It's a text from Nova.

> Nova: Three, huh? That's pretty rad. Did you just know that off the top of your head?

Of course Nova uses words like rad. That's how I would describe her, I think. She's rad.

> Casey: I did. The ocean is kind of my thing

> Nova: Tell me another fact

I rack my brain for any other facts that I remember reading from my childhood ocean encyclopedias.

> Casey: A blue whale's heart is the size of a small car

A minute later, she texts me back.

Nova: Are all of your ocean facts heart related?

I feel like I have something to prove to her now.

Casey: Jellyfish have been around for over 650 million years, predating dinosaurs and sharks

I'm finishing up the last chapter about an hour later when she texts me again.

Nova: Wow. Who would've thought something without a brain would be able to survive so long without going extinct? Maybe that's the problem with humans. We're too smart to survive

Casey: No argument here

At dinner, I'm a bit spaced out. Dad had us pray, as usual, but I barely remember what he said. My thoughts were and still are on my conversation with Nova. We've been texting here and there since I got home. I wasn't sure what to do with the paper with her number on it because throwing it away felt wrong, so I hid it.

"Casey." Dad is looking at me, a bit of barbecue chicken on his fork. By the look on his face, I know he's said my name more than once. "Why aren't you eating?"

I look down at my plate where I've eaten about half of what's on my plate. "I'm full," I say casually.

Dad looks at me for a minute, then takes what's left of the chicken from my plate and puts it on his own. "It's disrespectful for you not to eat the meal your mother made," he says.

Mom catches my eye. "You're not anorexic, are you?"

I have my hands in my lap and I'm picking at my fingernails. "No." She always does this, with everything. Nothing can be as it is on the surface. I think she's paranoid.

Dad scoffs. "Of course she's not. Anorexic girls are skinny." I hate it when he does that. If I had a problem, he'd ignore it. He treats me like I'm a child and not like I'm nearly 17.

In a little over a year, I'll be an adult and I can do what I want. He doesn't see that, though. He thinks I'm 6 years old and me having an opinion, or a different thought from him, is disrespectful since he's not only my dad but also a man. He does the same thing to my mom, but she just lets him.

I look at Mom instead. "Can I be excused, please? I still have some homework to finish."

"I didn't think a school like that would give so much homework," Mom says.

"They have to do something to keep the ghetto kids off the street, Stephanie. If they don't load those kids up with homework, they'll be in our neighborhood." My dad uses the word ghetto to mean black and brown kids. He's the type of person who thinks poor white kids can pick themselves up by the bootstraps, but black and brown kids are stuck in the cycle because they're not smart or disciplined.

Mom nods, agreeing with him. "Put your plate in the dishwasher and head on up," she says to me.

I do and head back up to my room where I go back to texting Nova.

2

Nova is leaned on the locker next to mine waiting on me. "You should have been there last night," she says as I unlock my locker. "The woman who spoke transitioned, like, twenty years ago in the 90s. She's so cool, dude. I wish you could have heard her speak." She's talking quickly and bouncing on her heels. "It really put a fire under me, you know?"

I hold my books to my chest and close my locker. "No. I have no idea what you're talking about."

She rolls her eyes at herself. "Right, sorry. The woman last night was talking about how at the Pride festival coming up, they don't really include transgender people, especially transgender people of color. She's going to be a part of the parade representing them. It just got me excited for Pride this year."

I can sense the exciting energy coming off of her and it's contagious because I'm excited for her. I lean toward her once we're sat in our seats in English class. "I think that's really cool. I hope she gets the attention she deserves."

At lunch, Kaida eyes me as I sit down. "Based on what Nova told me about your parents, you're not going to Pride this year?"

I can see that Nova didn't want Kaida to bring it up. "I've never been," I tell her.

She doesn't believe me. "Everyone goes, even if they're straight."

I don't argue her assumption that I'm straight. "My parents protest the festivals every year. I'm not allowed anywhere close."

J.J smirks, the butt of a cigarette hanging between their lips. "You're really a rule follower, aren't you? Have you ever stepped out of line, even once?"

Based on how my parents and their friends always talked about the LGBT community, I was deathly afraid of stepping out of line, even doing unrelated things. I'm terrified that if my parents found out, they'd send me away, like a boy I used to know was. I can't tell J.J or anyone else that, though, so I play up the vanilla girl they think I am.

"I've never had a reason to," I shrug.

Kaida is giving me a look like I'm the most boring person in the world. "You've never snuck off with a boyfriend or stolen some liquor from your dad's cabinet?"

There's a voice inside my head that's telling me to come out right now just so she stops assuming I'm straight. The other voice, the one that's louder, is telling me that they wouldn't accept me. It would be a repeat of Arizona. They would call me names or somehow, it would get back to my parents.

"I never had a reason to break the rules," I repeat, trying to keep the annoyance out of my voice. No guys were interested in me and with my friends in Arizona too disgusted to want to have to admit they were associated with me, no girls were lining up to kiss me either. I've had beers before, but it didn't taste nice, and drugs were never appealing to me.

Apparently, the annoyance came through in my voice because everyone but Lars is looking at me. Lars is, as usual, in his own world on his laptop. Nova touches her knee to mine. "So, pride," she says, getting the attention off of me. "Are we still taking the train into the city?"

In the last class of the day, Nova finds me by my locker. "Need a ride?"

I close my locker, holding the strap of my bag. "I take the bus, remember?"

One of her thick eyebrows lifts. "Do you want to take the bus?"

I can't imagine that anyone wants to take the bus and I make a face. "It smells bad and they're all so loud for no reason. Plus, the bus driver is kind of weird and I swear he smells like booze."

Now, both eyebrows are raised. "Is that a yes?" I nod. "Rad."

Nova's car is faded blue and probably older than we are. The door squeaks when I open it and I'm afraid to pull the door too hard in case it detaches from the rest of the car. The interior is a tan fabric that's also faded and there are small tears where I can see the stuffing. The fabric on the roof sags a little in places and there are cigarette burns, probably from the previous owner or J.J. I sit my bag between my feet since the backseat is full of random things like clothes and blankets. When Nova gets into the passenger seat, she throws her bag into the backseat with all the other stuff.

When she cranks the car, music blares from the speakers, which she quickly turns down to a decent volume. "Sorry, it's usually just me."

"It's fine." I gesture to the backseat. "You don't live in your car, do you?"

She laughs. "Of course not. I have a house. Technically, it's my grandparents' house, but I have a room there."

"So, what's with all the stuff?"

"It's there in case I run into someone who needs a coat or a blanket since I usually don't have cash on me. I have a couple sleeping bags in the trunk for when it gets really cold." She talks about it so casually, like it's something everyone does.

As she's been talking, I've been looking over the things in her backseat. "You just ride around and give people these things for free?"

She nods like it's obvious. "It's not like the government is helping them or anything. A lot of shelters in the city are full or they don't take in anyone who isn't in dire need when it's warm out. In the winter, there are people sleeping outside the shelters just in case the shelter has extra food or someone dies and a bed opens up." She shrugs. "The shelters run off donations, mostly, but no one thinks to give to them except around Christmas and that money only goes so far."

I turn back around to sit in the seat normally. "You're kind of amazing." I'd meant to keep that thought in my head and I talk again before she can say anything. "I didn't know about the shelters. My parents always had me work with the church back home around Christmas to help the homeless. We'd volunteer at soup kitchens and things like that, but I guess I never really thought about the rest of the year."

She starts driving in the direction I motion to my house. "That's the mentality of most people, unfortunately. I think it stems from childhood. Like, we tell kids that Santa is watching, but we only say that when it's close to Christmas. I've never heard a parent threaten to call Santa in July. I think adults think God is only watching them around Christmas, too, so they only care when God's watching, in a sense."

I motion which turns to take. "At my old church, it was like it was a competition, especially with older people. It was as if they wanted to get on God's good side before they died, so they'd give the most money or wrap the most gifts for the kids in whatever third world country. The kids or the homeless didn't matter to them. All that mattered was that they were the best Christians and made everyone else feel inferior."

Nova laughs. "Faith is such a strange thing."

Over our texting conversation last night, Nova has learned about my parents, and since my mom works from home, Nova knows that she can't be seen by either of my parents. She'd sort of laughed it off last night when I said it, but I think it hurt her to be rejected by people who don't know her. Normally, I'd have kept that sort of thing to myself, but there's something about speaking via a screen that makes things easier to say.

"Where do you want me to drop you?" Nova asks me once we turn onto my road.

I point to the side of the road before we get to the hill

that leads around a bend to my house. "Here is fine."

She looks down the street once we've parked. "Should you wait until your bus passes before you go in?"

As much as I try to get the details of my life right, I slip up. I know what to say to my parents and what not to say to everyone else, but simple paranoias slip my mind. I don't think humans were meant to be carrying so many versions of themselves inside their heads all at once.

I settle back into the seat. "Yeah, good idea."

She puts the car in park and sits back in the seat casually. She looks at me. "I feel like I need to keep apologizing for Kaida. She basically says whatever she's thinking."

I'd put the whole thing with Kaida out of my mind. Everyone assumes I'm straight, probably partly because I've given them no reason to think otherwise, but also because that's the default, isn't it? Girls like boys. Boys like girls. It all seems so simple until you realize it's not.

"It's fine," I shrug. "No big deal."

She reaches over to me and I think she's going to hold my hand, but then her fingers graze my wrist as she brings my hand from my mouth where I've nervously been biting on the side of my thumb. Her hand lingers over where she's released my wrist and then she takes her hand back. I think she's asking me with her eyes if what she's done is okay. She's asking my permission to touch me after she's touched me.

"Thanks," I grin. "I hardly realize when I'm doing it."

"I get it. It took me years to stop chewing on the ends of my hair. I read this story somewhere where some girl died and they found balls of her hair in her stomach and colon. I think it was bullshit, but it scared me enough to stop."

Her story makes me laugh and she smiles too at how ridiculous the story is. I look down at the pink skin of my thumb. "I tried to scare myself out of it once. I told myself I'd get sick from the germs on my hands."

"It obviously didn't work."

"No, it didn't," I laugh. "I figured out that it was either

this or hurting myself. A stupid cold didn't seem as bad after that."

I see her eyes go to my forearms, but she won't find any marks there. She won't find marks anywhere because the good thing about fingernails is that the tiny crescents don't stay long, not if you control the pressure.

Her eyes flick up to mine. "I'd have to agree."

I've never found it easy to talk to someone before. Maybe it's that Nova isn't the type to judge, or maybe it's that I know she has her own pain she's not talking about, but something about her makes me want to be open. I want to tell her. If anyone would understand my fear of coming out, she would, right?

"If I tell you something, do you promise you won't laugh?"

A crease appears in between her eyebrows. "Is it another ocean fact?" She's teasing me. She must see that I'm serious because of how her face softens. "Okay, I promise."

I can feel my heart threatening to beat through my chest. My hands are starting to feel moist and I'm aware of the way my thumb seems to gravitate to my teeth. "I, uh…" I hear the bus come around the corner and it passes on Nova's side. I panic. I can't tell her. She won't understand, not like I want her to. She'll react like my friends in Arizona did, or she'll think I'm trying to impress her. "I should go."

As I reach for the door with one hand on my bag, her words make me pause. "What were you going to tell me?"

I reach through my scrambled brain for anything to grasp onto. "I'm glad we're friends," I finally say.

She looks confused. "Yeah, me too."

"Text me when you get home," I say as I climb from the car.

3

It's been a week since I met Nova, and since I haven't been able to hang out with her outside of school, we've been texting when we're not around each other. Last night, she'd asked me something I didn't expect—to not only drive me home from school like she has been this past week but to drive me in the mornings, too. Last night, my heart jumped into my throat at the idea of having more time alone with Nova. I tried to play it cool, waiting about a minute before replying, but then I'd said YES in all capital letters, so that didn't go as planned.

I'm only standing outside for a few minutes when I see her car come around the corner. I can hear her music playing, but she has it at a reasonable level. As she's been driving me home after school, she plays it a little loud if she doesn't feel like talking, and I watch as her head bobs up and down and she beats the steering wheel along with the drums. Every time she whisper-sings the words, I think about how cute she is and I'm jealous that she doesn't seem nervous around me.

"I might have my own car soon," I tell her as I put my seatbelt on. Dad had mentioned it in passing before we moved here. "So, you won't have to drive me around much longer."

She pulls away from the street and makes a three-point turn to go away from my house. She turns the music down until it's just a hum over the speakers. "If I didn't want to do this, I wouldn't have offered."

It's obvious to me that by 'this' she means to drive me to and from school, but for a second I think by 'this' she means spending time alone with me. "I just don't want to harsh your vibe if you wanted some time alone to listen to your music, or whatever."

Her eyes crinkle in the outer corners as she laughs like they always do. "'Harsh my vibe'? Who talks like that?" She glances at me. "My older brother is away in college, so it's just me and my grandparents in my house. Believe me, any conversation with anyone under the age of sixty is a nice change."

"I didn't know you had an older brother."

"Jessie. He's a sophomore down at Georgia Tech. I guess you're an only child?"

Back in Arizona, everyone knew about my little brother and I never had to say it out loud, but now, things are different. "Technically. When I was seven, I had a little brother that was stillborn."

"I'm sorry. That really sucks."

Having a stillborn child really messed up my mom and she had to go to therapy for a long time. Dad kept trying to get her to have more kids, but after she had a couple of miscarriages post-Noah, the doctors made her stop before it killed her.

I don't tell Nova any of this. She already knows about my relationship with my parents and she knows my dad and I don't really get along. I don't need her thinking he's abusive or anything. "Thanks." I change the subject. "So, why do you live with your grandparents?"

We're in the parking lot of the school now. She sits in silence for so long that I nearly apologize for bringing it up, but then runs a hand through her hair, like she's thinking. "My dad was killed while my mom was pregnant with me. He was a security guard in the city. Someone shot him by accident thinking he was someone else as they drove by a club. My mom tried to raise me and Jesse on her own, but she didn't have the money and she had all these mental illnesses stacked up, which made her really depressed and paranoid. When I was one and Jesse was three, she dropped us at her parents' house, then took off."

I fidget with my fingers in my lap, unsure of what to say. "I'm sorry I brought it up. I didn't mean to make you think about that stuff."

She side-eyes me, grinning. "I don't mind. That's what friends do."

I pretend to scratch the side of my nose to hide my smile. "Can I ask you one more question, then? You don't have to answer if it's too personal."

"She's dead, too," she says solemnly. She already knew what I was going to ask. "She overdosed on her meds in a motel room in Texas."

Before I realize what I'm doing, my hand is on her arm, softly holding onto her wrist. I take my hand away as quickly as I put it there, crossing my arms over my chest instead. I decide to tell her about Noah, but I leave out the part about my dad.

When I'm done, her eyes flick down to the cupholders beneath the radio. "Death sucks, huh?"

I appreciate the way she's able to sum things up, even serious things. "Yeah, it does."

♀

It's Friday night and while I know everyone else in my school is out with their friends, probably at a party somewhere, I'm up in my room doing some homework. It's pushing midnight and my parents have been asleep for a while, something I know I should be, but the overachiever in me has my brain working in overtime. Needing a break, I check my phone and see that Nova texted me a minute ago.

Nova: I'm outside

I frantically text her back, jumping up from my seat.

Casey: Why? Then: I can't go outside. The doors have alarms

A few minutes pass and I think she's gone back home or to join up with the others. Maybe she thought I'd go with her and now she's disappointed. I know there's nothing I can do, so I go back to my homework. Suddenly, there's a tapping on my bedroom window, which makes my body tense for a moment.

I raise the blinds and see Nova crouched on the roof of my front porch, waving. I open the window slowly. "What are you doing?" I whisper. I look past her into the dark yard below the window. "How did you get up here?"

She grins. "I have my ways." She looks me over. "Cute pajamas."

I glance down at my light pink cotton shorts and a matching t-shirt. "Get in here before you fall and break your neck," I say as I step back from the window, letting her in. I close the window once she's inside.

When I turn around, she has a cross in her hand from my dresser—one of many. "At least no vampires will come in," she jokes.

I take the cross from her. "My mom put them there." I put the cross back. "You never told me what you're doing here," I remind her.

She continues to look around. The only light in my room is coming from my desk lamp. With her black clothes, she looks like a shadow in the faintly lit room. She picks up my childhood basketball trophy from when I played for the YMCA.

"I wanted to see you," she says casually. "And I knew you wouldn't be able to leave because of your dictators, so I came to you." She turns the trophy over in her hands, reading it. "Most Improved. I didn't figure you for the sporty type."

I try not to think too much about her comment that she wanted to see me tonight. "We lost every game. Those trophies were given to us for participating."

She laughs quietly. "At least you're honest." She puts the trophy back.

"I never really cared," I shrug. "My dad was a jock and since I'm his only kid, I didn't really have a choice when it came to playing sports."

She motions over to my desk. "Did I interrupt your homework?"

"Just math."

She fakes a yawn and walks over to my bed, which is right

next to the desk. She takes her boots off and lays on my bed, her back propped on my headboard. "You can finish it."

I sit back in the desk chair. In two movements, I could be on my bed with her, but I don't move. I hold my pencil casually. "You don't have to stay if you're going to be bored. I'm sure you have better things to do than hang out with me on a Friday night."

She doesn't move. "Not really," she smirks. She looks around my room. "Do you have anything I can sketch in?"

I open my desk drawer and pull out a sketchbook and some pencils. "I went through a phase a couple of years ago where I thought I was going to be an artist, but then I realized I can't draw." I hand her the book and pencils. "These are brand new."

She looks over the book and pencils, then gives me a look like I've said something ridiculous. "They're really nice." She looks back at my desk. "You concentrate on your work. Don't mind me." She flips open the book and starts sketching.

I do as she says, but it's hard to concentrate with her sitting cross-legged on my bed, her hair tucked behind her ear as she concentrates. I keep stealing glances at her, admiring how beautiful she is.

"What are you sketching?" I ask a few minutes later.

She flicks her eyes over to me. "It's a surprise. I'm almost done."

I nod and continue my work. When I'm done, I put my books back into my book bag. By the direction she's holding the pencil, I can tell she's working on the shading. I attempt to peek over. "When can I see it?"

She looks over her work before handing me the book. "Go easy," she says. "I'm sensitive," she smirks.

The sketch is of me just now, doing my homework. I'm biting at my thumb in concentration in her sketch. I can't believe how accurately she's drawn me. "You even put the freckles on my arm." I look at the detail of how my shorts fall across my thigh. "Nova, this is amazing."

"It's not my best," she shrugs, resting her elbows on her knees.

"Can I keep it?"

She's taken back in surprise. "I was going to trash it," she stammers.

I go over to the bed and sit next to her, then give her the book again. "Sign it for me."

She looks down at the sketch. "Seriously?"

I nod and she takes the book from me. She signs the bottom right corner and then gives it back. I rip the page carefully from the book. "Now, when you're famous, I can say that I have a Nova M original."

She grins nervously, spinning the pencil in her hand. "I'll never be a famous artist."

I hold up the sketch. "I beg to differ. This is the best sketch I've ever seen."

She's biting on the middle of her lip, her lip ring clicking against her teeth. "If you say so." She goes to hand me the sketchbook back.

"Keep it. I want to see what you do with it."

Her eyes are searching mine, confused, but appreciative. "Thank you."

I can feel myself starting to blush from the thoughts going through my head. My eyes go to her lips. I want to kiss her. This is the perfect chance to tell her how I feel. It's quiet around us and the room is only dimly lit by my lamp. The moment is romantic and intimate, just like I imagined the perfect moment would be when I told her the truth. Those thoughts are suddenly interrupted by the intrusive thoughts of having to out myself. The fears crawling through my brain make everything in my vision go sharp instead of soft and romantic. It's too dark in here now, and we're too close.

I stand suddenly from the bed, her sketch still in my hand. "I should put this somewhere safe."

I go over to my desk and find tacks and the piece of paper Nova had written her number on the first day we met. I take both pieces of paper and enough tacks to my closet. I move my clothes aside to show the blank white wall behind them. I tack Nova's sketch and the paper with her number to the wall. When I'm satisfied that both pieces are secure, I turn back to Nova for approval.

She stays sat on my bed as she eyes my closet wall. "A secret," she says flatly.

I slide my clothes back over the wall, hiding it from plain sight. "It's nothing personal. It's just…"

Nova is still watching me with those curious eyes. "No, I understand." She sits on the edge of the bed and slides her boots on. "I should go." She grabs the sketchbook and pencils. "Thanks for these," she says as she goes to the window.

I meet her at the window with a purple tote bag from my closet. "This will make it easier to carry when you're somehow climbing down my roof."

She looks over the tote, which is one my mom made years ago with a Paul quote on it and some decorative crosses. She gives me a look before she puts her things in it. "I'll give this back to you tomorrow."

"Don't worry about it. Add it to the collection in your backseat. Someone will find a good use for it."

"Good idea." She opens the window. "See you later."

I stand in the window as she quietly steps to the other side. "Text me when you're home."

She turns back and smiles at me before she walks across my roof. I watch her as she slides down the roof and dangles from it. She must drop to the railing of the porch because I don't see her for a few seconds until she's walking across my yard. In the streetlights, I see her wave back at me from the sidewalk. I wave back and once she's out of my line of vision, I close the window back and let the blinds down.

As I lay in bed after cutting the lights, I can smell where she was leaned back against my pillow. It's not a discernible smell. I couldn't recreate it into a perfume or anything, but it's her. I lay with the side of my face against the pillow so I can fall asleep to her smell. I begin to wonder what would have happened if I kissed her tonight. My initial thought is that she would have probably freaked out and would've left in a hurry. My second thought, though, the one I hope would have been true, is that she would've kissed me back.

4

    It's Saturday afternoon, a week since Nova snuck up to my room, and things between me and Nova feel different now like we broke some kind of barrier when she came to my room. Since that night, I've felt her open up to me more. She's also touching me more, in a casual way. She doesn't hesitate anymore when she brings my hand from my mouth or when she bumps against me as we walk the halls. My favorite thing she does is when she makes me laugh in English class by being a complete dork. When we were given scissors for a book project, she pretended to cut her whole finger off, flailing silently next to me. She does that a lot—makes an idiot out of herself in front of people. I like to think it's to make me laugh, which it does, but maybe she just likes the attention.

I'm up in my room putting away laundry in my closet, admiring Nova's sketch, when I get a text. Nova's name flashes across my screen and my heart skips a beat.

Nova: I know this is kind of last minute, but there's a show tonight in the city. FOOD TRUCKS. Can you can sneak out?

Being invited along to something Nova and her friends usually do by themselves feels nice like I'm finally being accepted. I know it's Nova's idea. Around her friends, she's been pulling me into conversations, making me feel included, and like my opinion on something matters. I'm starting to feel like I have a place amongst her and her friends, and not so much like I'm the outcast amongst the group of outcasts.

    Casey: How?

Nova: I didn't expect that answer. Think of any reason to stay in your room all night. I'll pick you up at our spot at 8

After I agree to this plan, I go through my closet looking for anything black. All the black clothes I have are ones I've worn to funerals, and are probably a little too churchy for a concert. I grab a short-sleeved white shirt instead. I go to my desk drawer and find a thick black sharpie from where I marked up the boxes for my room when we moved. I lay the white shirt on the floor and sit on my knees as I write a phrase I'd seen on a sticker on the back of Lars's laptop. While the shirt dries, I find a pair of old jeans that have some holes in the knees and frayed bottoms. I don't have any boots or cool sneakers, so I'm stuck with my flats.

Before I go down for dinner, I come up with a plan on what to tell my parents. I have to be convincing and give them no reason to check on me for the rest of the night. I spritz some water on my face and throw a blanket over my pajama-clad body before I go downstairs, hunched over for added pity. I cough and sniffle loud enough for my parents to hear as I descend the stairs and go into the kitchen.

When Mom sees me, she rushes over. "Casey, what's wrong?"

I've been upstairs most of the day, to my advantage. I pretend that I'm having a hard time talking. "I'm sick," I say pitifully, touching my throat.

She puts her hand to my forehead. "You are a little warm and you're covered in sweat." She wipes the back of her hand on her jeans before she goes to the medicine cabinet in the kitchen.

She's looking through the medicines. "What do you think it is, a cold? The flu?"

I swallow. "I just need rest," I assure her. "Some kids at my school have this too. It's a short bug. I'll be fine."

"Joyce hasn't mentioned Patrick getting sick, but maybe he got lucky." She looks me over. "Can you at least take some Tylenol?" I nod. She shakes two pills into my hand and gives me a glass of water.

When she turns to focus on dinner, I pocket the pills and sip the water. "Can I go upstairs and sleep now?" I keep the pitiful tone in my voice as if I'm a small child again.

This tugs on her mother heartstrings and she nods. "I'll be up later to check on you."

I can feel a panic in my chest that my plan is going to unravel. "I don't want to get you sick. The church needs you tomorrow. I'll just be sleeping. I won't even know you're there."

She thinks this over. I know she's leading some projects at church, including her involvement of protesting Pride, which I try not to think about. Finally, she sighs. "You're right. I don't know how the WBSG has survived this long without me."

I nod, pretending to agree, and slowly head back up the stairs. My parents have no reason to suspect that I'm lying. I've never snuck out before. I've never had to. With the friends I had back in Arizona, I had no reason to lie to my parents when I'd go out with them. My friends would party sometimes, which I didn't usually attend, but most of the time, it was just our group at someone's house or at the mall. I never imagined I would be going to a punk show with a girl I have a crush on.

When it's close to time to meet Nova, I pull on a black tank top, then the rest of the clothes I set out earlier. The text I wrote on the shirt earlier goes straight across my boobs, which only emphasizes the message. I line my eyes in black eyeliner and smudge it a little. I don't know anything about punk fashion besides what I've seen from Nova and her friends, so I don't really know what I'm doing. I leave my hair down since I don't have any temporary dye, and I need to look normal tomorrow morning when I'm dragged to Sunday Service. I look myself over in the mirror and hope that what I've done is good enough.

I lock my bedroom door and cut the lights before I attempt to sneak out. The sun has gone down recently, so the sky is still the slightest bit navy. I step through the window and pull down the blinds from the other side before quietly closing the window back. Like I saw Nova do the other day, I half crouch as I walk across the roof of the porch, keeping my steps close together. I'm half crawling by the time I reach the point of the roof that rounds the side of the house where Nova had dropped down. I look down at the ground and figure that even if I fell, I would be okay. Maybe a little bruised, but that would go along with the whole punk thing, I think. I carefully turn and back up to the edge of the roof. In one swift motion, I lower myself so that I'm hanging by my hands. My toes find the railing of the porch and I let go of the roof, finding the post to hold onto.

I can see that the light in the living room is still on and the TV is flickering against the blinds. I climb down the porch and when my feet hit the ground, I turn and jog a little until I can't see my house from the sidewalk. The adrenaline from sneaking out of my house for the first time carries me until I'm over the hill. Once I see Nova's car, the nerves erupt in me and I start to think I look like an idiot since this outfit is not my normal garb. I consider taking the top shirt off and tossing it into the trees before I get to the car. She's already seen me, though, because she waves when I get close.

When I slide into the passenger seat and close the door, the car goes dark around us. Nova reaches up and flicks the cab light on. "What does your shirt say?"

I can feel myself blushing and I'm glad I put on a little more makeup than usual tonight. I move my hair back and pull the shirt down to make the letters readable. "Nazi punks, fuck off," I read shyly. I sit normally and pull the seatbelt over me. "It's stupid, isn't it?"

She laughs. "Not at all. I think it's cool."

I tuck my hair behind my ear. "Thanks." I see her grin as she flicks the light off again.

♀

Nova pulls into the parking lot of an old building about twenty minutes later. As we'd pulled closer to the place, I could see multiple brick buildings that look industrial along with some apartments I think would be cool to live in. The parking lot we've parked in is nearly full and it takes a few minutes for her to find a spot. I can see from here that there's a sizable crowd in front of the outdoor stage, which looks nearly set up. There aren't any concert lights yet, but only street lights above the venue which extend out to the parking lot and the other buildings.

I unlatch my seatbelt and open the car door to leave the car when Nova's hand on my arm stops me. "Wait." I look back at her. I can see her face now in the light of the cab light. Her hand comes to my face and her thumb wipes by the outer corner of my eye. "Mascara flake," she says as she takes her hand back. The curious look is back on her face.

"Thanks." There's a beat of silence and my eyes flick toward the crowd. "Should we go?"

She blinks and comes back to this moment. "Yeah, let's go."

I follow her across the parking lot and to the main area. The food trucks she mentioned in her text line the entryway on either side. The walkway is crowded with people waiting to order food, their conversations blending together. They're all dressed similarly and I realize that at the moment, I actually fit in, kind of. I have this feeling of eyes on me, but I'm not sure if anyone is actually looking at me. I feel like a poser and I wish I would've stuck with the black tank top sans homemade shirt.

"See anything you want?" Nova asks me, bringing me out of my thoughts.

I look around at the different trucks. "I've never had food from a truck."

She looks surprised, but she doesn't make a comment. "It's the best. You have to try the sweet potato tacos from the vegetarian truck. They have a sauce they put on top that has some lime in it. It's amazing."

She stops at one of the trucks, Linda's Legumes, which is painted yellow with a giant green leaf on the side. Nova takes the lead once we get through the line. She orders us two orders of the sweet potato tacos and two bottled drinks. After the girl puts in the order, Nova goes for her pocket.

I put my hand on her arm. "I got it." I pull out a twenty and hand it to the girl before Nova can argue. I donate the change into the tip jar just inside the window.

Nova and I stand to the side to wait on our food. She nudges me. "You didn't have to pay. I asked you here, remember?"

I grin. "I know."

After we get our food, I follow Nova to a section of the area where tables are set up. The tables are all taken, but Nova and I see the rest of the group at the same time over by a short wall. J.J and Kaida are sat on the wall while Lars is sat in his chair. They've already gotten their food.

"Yo," Kaida says as Nova sits next to her on the wall. I sit next to Nova.

"Yo," Nova echoes.

Kaida looks around Nova at me. "Someone grew a set. How'd you get out of Guantanamo Bay?"

"Faked the plague," I tell her.

J.J looks at me too. "Cool shirt." They take a drag off of their cigarette. "It's even cooler that it's so obviously hand made."

I can't tell if they're insulting my t-shirt or not. "Thanks," I say flatly.

Nova glances at me. "I kind of miss the blouses," she says casually.

I can't read her tone either, so I change the subject instead. I notice that Lars doesn't have a screen in front of him and is instead somewhat paying attention to what's going on around him as he eats something double fried on a stick.

"I don't think I've ever seen you without your laptop," I tell him.

"We're not at school." He pops one of the fried balls into his mouth. "I find school dull and a waste of my time. Everyone knows the future is going straight tech, so I code instead of whatever bullshit I'm supposed to be paying attention to."

I take a sip of my water. "How do you pass your classes?"

"Lars is a genius," J.J says. "He doesn't have to pay attention to pass the class."

"It's common sense," Lars says flippantly. "It takes more effort to fail."

Nova looks at me and rolls her eyes at Lars's comment, which makes me laugh quietly. She smiles too. A flash goes off, which brings our attention to Kaida. She looks down at her phone screen. "That's such a good picture. I'll send it to you," she tells Nova. "Casey, give me your number and I'll send it to you too." She hands me her phone. After I enter my number and give her back her phone, she taps her screen. "Cool. Got it."

I feel my phone buzz in my pocket that I've received the picture. I want to check it, but I don't. I'm afraid I'll look different in the photo and I'm not sure I want to look at myself right now if I look stupid and no one wants to tell me. I don't want to break the illusion of being liked by seeing myself the way everyone else is seeing me.

After we've finished eating, we all head toward the stage. People move out of the way so that Lars can get a spot toward the side of the stage in order to see the band and not just see the backs of people.

I go to follow J.J and Kaida as they join Lars, but Nova puts her hand on my arm, stopping me. "Stay here." We're stood within the rest of the crowd. "This is where the excitement is." She drops her hand from my arm when I stand next to her.

The band comes out on the stage and everyone erupts into cheers. The lead singer goes to the mic and she starts talking about the government, which she suggests burning to the ground. She talks about oppression and racism within this city, which I didn't realize was a thing. She finishes her talk with damning the construction of a housing community a couple of blocks over, which means the concerts here are going to have to be done by 10 pm once people move in. She starts a call and response with the audience that I'm too shy to join, but Nova raises her voice with the others.

The music begins, which ends the call and response. The singer starts singing, which could almost be a very loud spoken word with electric guitar and drums going behind her. Everyone around us starts jumping, Nova along with them. I'm still standing still because I'm unsure of what to do.

Nova turns to me, still jumping, and grabs my shoulders. "Just bounce," she instructs over the music.

I hold onto her shoulders and we bounce together to the music. A minute later, a circle opens in the middle of the crowd and Nova pulls me back from it. Some people rush to the empty circle and start shoving each other and swinging their arms.

I lean over toward Nova, still bouncing on the balls of my feet. "What are they doing?" I have to yell over the music and the cheers from everyone else.

"Moshing," she informs me.

"It seems very primal."

She laughs. "It is."

We continue to bounce and watch the moshing going on in the middle of the crowd. Some people are walking away with bloody noses and black eyes, but they're laughing and putting their arms up in victory as they leave the circle. Nova nudges me and points to the side of the stage where some muscular people, including J.J, are holding up Lars in his chair as I've seen in movies about Jewish weddings. The singer of the band notices this and I see her smile, holding out a fist to Lars. If this group of people is anything, they're inclusive.

It seems like a long time later when I have to take a break. I motion to Nova that I'm headed out of the crowd and she nods before she grabs my hand and leads me through the tightly packed crowd who are jumping and bumping into each other. She continues to hold my hand until we're out of the crowd. When she drops my hand, I nearly reach out to take it again. She hands me a cup of water from a complimentary water station. "I'm impressed with how you're holding up," she breathes.

I'm still breathing a bit heavy and I can feel the sweat on

the back of my neck. "How often do you do this?"

She grabs her own water cup. "As much as I can. The summer is popular for these kinds of shows, but in the winter, it all kind of dies down and we have to find some underground show in some random person's basement."

I sip my water. "That seems kind of dangerous."

"It's not. Everyone is really respectful and chill. If anyone tries to come into the group and act predatory or be a dick in general, they're ostracized from any of the events."

I look back toward the show, which hasn't lost any energy since the start. "With all the pushing and shoving, I'm surprised there hasn't been a real fight."

"That's the whole point. Opening a pit like that is an opportunity for everyone who needs it to get their aggression out in a fun way. It may not look like it, but they have complete control over their bodies. They're letting the music fuel them and basically dumping that energy out in a nondestructive way."

I finish the water. "So, it's therapeutic for them?"

She nods. "A lot of these people don't come from the best home lives. They're oppressed or feel unwelcome at home, so they come here to feel like they belong. This community is like their own family for them."

A while later, Kaida, J.J, and Lars find me and Nova back at the picnic tables from earlier sipping on water and talking about the show. J.J lights up a cigarette. "How'd you do, newbie?"

"She was great," Nova says. "No one even noticed that this was her first show."

Lars wipes his sweaty hands on his pants. "I should probably head home. I have a program running tonight and I need to see if it was successful or not."

J.J flicks the ash off their cigarette. "Okay. I should probably get home too. Mom's working a double and I left the twelve-year-old to watch the five-year-old."

Kaida looks at me and smiles. "It was cool of you to show up tonight. You'll have to come out with us again."

I nod. "Depending on how successful I am getting back into my house tonight, I'd love to."

Nova stands too. "Speaking of, I should probably get you home," she says to me. "It's late."

The five of us walk back through the food trucks and to the parking lot where Nova and I break off and go toward the back since we got here later than them. When we get into Nova's car, she cranks the A.C.

I fan my shirt out and lean back against the headrest. "It's disgusting how sweaty I am right now," I laugh.

She laughs with me. "That's part of the fun."

Nova pulls the car over to the side of the street at our usual spot. As she drove, I grew more and more anxious about not only being away from her for the night but also having to sneak back into my house. I look toward the direction of my house, hoping my parents haven't noticed that I'm gone.

"I'm starting to think sneaking out was the easy part," I say, undoing my seatbelt.

"It sucks that you have to go home at all. My grandparents wouldn't care if you stayed the night."

I stop breathing for a moment thinking about spending the night with Nova, sharing her bed. "It's probably safer if I sneak back in, honestly. My parents would flip worse if they found out I spent the night somewhere."

"Are you sure you want to wear that shirt, in case they catch you sneaking in?"

I look down at my shirt, remembering what I wrote. "Oh, you're right." I start pulling it off. "Do you mind keeping this for me?"

She's watching me. "No, I don't mind." I take the shirt off and she takes it. She haphazardly folds it and puts it next to her between her hip and the door. "I'll bring it to school on Monday."

I exhale, feeling much cooler in just my tank top. "If I make it to Monday," I half joke.

Her hand grazes my arm as I leave. "Text me when you

get in."

I ignore the goosebumps from where her fingers touched my skin. "Okay, but don't check your phone until you get stopped."

She sarcastically salutes me. "Yes, ma'am."

I walk around to the side of the house where I climbed down earlier avoiding the windows in case one of my parents is still awake downstairs. I carefully get up on the railing of the porch and curl my fingers around the roof above me. I have no idea how Nova did this the other day. Did she shimmy up the gutter? Did she pull herself up that far? I choose to try the latter. Pulling myself up and relying solely on my upper body strength isn't working. I consider calling Nova and telling her I've had a change of heart about getting into my room tonight, but I know that's not an option.

I grip the roof harder and jump off the railing, which allows me to pull myself to the roof. I awkwardly roll myself on my shoulder, scraping the skin as I lay on my back. I sit up slowly and crawl on my hands and knees until I'm beneath my window. I sit up on my knees and use my palms to slide the window up by the glass until I can get my fingers underneath it. Once the window is completely up, I find the string to the blinds and raise those too. My room is still dark and my door is closed, which is a good sign. I step through the window and shut it behind me. I flick on the lamp on my desk to an empty room.

I exhale, relieved, as I close the blinds, then tiptoe across my room to put pajamas on.

After I'm changed, I get the makeup off of my face and climb into my bed. I flick the desk lamp off and grab my phone from my desk where I plugged it in. I send Nova a text, as promised.

Casey: Safe and sound

About ten minutes later, she texts me back.

Nova: No sign that they noticed?

Casey: If they even suspected I was somewhere I wasn't supposed to be, they'd have called the police and put up missing posters

I'm looking at the picture Kaida sent me of me and Nova. I don't look bad in the picture and Nova looks amazing as usual in her usual patched pants and vest over her t-shirt. We're smiling at each other as we're holding our food in our laps. My phone buzzes, interrupting the thoughts of contentment.

Nova: Awesome. That means you can come out with me more. Goodnight, Casey

My stomach flutters at the idea of going out with Nova again. Obviously, we're only friends, but I like being with her, especially getting to see what she's like outside of school, though it's not that much different. I think of her hand in mine, sweaty and not that romantic, but it was nice, nonetheless.

Casey: Goodnight, Nova

5

It's the smell of breakfast that wake me up, and I remember it's Sunday. I would have to be in the hospital to miss church this morning, and I'm glad my throat is a little sore from last night since I'm supposed to be getting over being sick. When I go downstairs after showering and putting on my church blouse, I sit at the kitchen table. Dad is already there with a Sunday paper covering his face. Something about not being able to see his face makes me nervous.

I sit on my hands. "Anything interesting?" I ask.

Dad flips the paper down to look at me. By the look on his face, I know I asked something I shouldn't have. "That man is ruining the damn country. He doesn't respect our military and he makes a mockery of the American values. Did you know that he's a Muslim? What kind of country are we if we don't have a good president with Christian values?"

My only option is to nod casually, hoping it's enough. "Mom made cinnamon rolls. The icing is my favorite part." He hasn't yelled at me or let on that he knows I snuck out, so I write his silence off as a win. "I'm glad I can eat them now that I'm not sick," I add for seemingly no reason.

He flips the paper back up to cover his face. He's only going to make himself more upset by reading that thing, but I'm not going to be the one to tell him that. Mom comes into the dining room a few minutes later and sets the cinnamon rolls down on the table.

"Those raccoons woke me up last night," she yawns.

"Raccoons?" I ask.

Dad folds his paper and sets it down next to his plate

while Mom serves him the rolls. "Late last night," she says. "It sounded like big ones too."

I'm the only one who realizes that they weren't raccoons on the roof last night, but me climbing back into my window. "Wow. I guess I was sleeping too deep to hear them." I serve myself rolls once Mom is done serving Dad.

Dad reaches his hand for mine to pray. "I'm going to put some of those poison pellets up there for them for the next time they get on the roof. That'll teach them."

I grab his hand as he grabs Mom's hand. "Won't that kill them?" I point out.

"We can only hope," he says with zero emotion.

The church was how it always is. We stood up a million times during the sermon to break for a hymn and then sat back down for more preaching. The only difference with today was that, with Pride coming up, the preacher had gone on a tirade mentioning more than once that the church needed volunteers for the protest. He then went on and on about how it's our job to show sinners to the light and all that. I tuned out most of it, biting my thumb until I could taste blood, and hoping I wasn't acting weird. When his eyes landed on mine, I held my breath as I desperately tried not to look guilty. When he looked away, I'd imagined what Nova would do if she heard the awful things he said about 'the gays' and 'the trannies'. Nova would've stood up and cussed him out. She would've gone up to the pulpit and rallied against all the hate. Love thy neighbor and all that. I'd sat in the pew wishing I had her bravery.

As I sat up in my room finishing a paper after, I wasn't upset at the preacher for what he said because of anything to do with faith. I've met loving Christians who accept everyone and want nothing more than to show love. I was upset with the preacher because he's hateful and he was preaching this hate to the congregation, including little kids. That's how the cycle continues. They can make as many LGBT movies as they want, and I support them, but when it's our own communities and families preaching hate, how can we believe that things get better for us? The reality is, the endings for us are likely to be much different than they're portrayed.

I'm sitting quietly at dinner while Dad basically regurgitates everything the preacher said this morning. I should be hungry, but I'm not. My stomach feels tight with the hatred that is being shoved down my throat. Hearing my dad say such bigoted things about the LGBT community, and unknowingly me, makes me feel even more ostracized in my own family than I already do. I know my parents would never accept me and they'd probably lose their love for me if I were to ever be out, but there's something that hits a little too close to home when they're talking about how disgusting I am. They wish I could be punished by the law for something as innocent as love. They wish I was dead, just so they didn't have to see it.

I only poke around at my food, wishing I wasn't here. My father's words wash over me like a black wave and I dig my thumbnail into the flesh of my finger to keep myself from crying, reminding myself that I can't let them see that I have anything to hide. Some people would say that people who hate gay people this much have something to hide, like a secret attraction to the same sex, but I don't think so in my father's case. Some people are just bullies, not because they're miserable or because they feel guilty about something, but just because they're not good people. I could try to give my father more love. I could try to somehow get him to change his mind by showing him pictures of gay couples with kids or show him that all love is good love, but it wouldn't help, and it's not my responsibility to make him love me.

I haven't heard from Nova much today and all I want to do is call her and hear her voice. I want to tell her everything. Maybe not that I like her, but maybe my secret. I want to tell her everything I've heard today from my preacher and my own dad. My mom didn't audibly echo my dad's thoughts, but she nodded along, which is just as bad. I nearly call Nova when I'm back upstairs, but I stop myself. I'm not special for having bigoted parents. A lot of kids do. What's going on with me isn't worth involving Nova. It would be selfish to put that on her. She didn't ask to take on my problems. I'll do what I've done for the past couple of years and shove it down.

♀

As soon as I see Nova on Monday morning waiting in her car for me, I feel like there's a light that clicks on inside of me and I smile, a real smile, as I slide into the passenger seat. I didn't know that seeing a person could make me feel so safe. It's like, if I can see Nova, even in a crowd of thousands, I know I'm safe. I know that every negative thought I've had lately about myself is wrong because she makes me feel like what I'm feeling is okay.

"So, I forgot your shirt," she says. "My grandma thought it was mine and she threw it in the dryer as to not mess up the ink. I'll get it back to you soon, though."

"Keep it," I shrug. "It's not like it's safe at my house."

"Okay," she smiles. "I'll keep it safe."

By the time lunch rolls around, there's this weight on my chest that has seemingly come out of nowhere and has radiated up my shoulders. Thinking back, I know what's triggered it. Patrick, the kid who goes to my church, brought up the sermon from yesterday in the hallway. He preached the same thing the preacher did, bringing the attention to himself. He pointedly called some other kid in the hallway a 'faggot', which was somehow not heard by any of the teachers. I'd tried to offer the targeted kid a sympathetic look, but there wasn't much I could do without outing myself, and that made me feel guilty because I shouldn't care if I'm outed, but I did.

I take deep breaths now, trying to not only alleviate this guilt but also to calm down the panic in my chest before I meet my friends at the table. Unsurprisingly, Kaida is talking about Pride, just like everyone is in one way or another. The school seems to be split on their opinion of the festival, but thankfully, no one has asked me my opinion on the festival or really included me in any conversation at all. Hanging with Nova has kept the conservative kids from talking to me, but the way I dress has kept pretty much everyone else from talking to me too. Kaida brings me into the conversation when I sit down. "We were just talking about Pride. How are you going to sneak out during the day?"

I shrug as I take a bite of my pizza. I don't really feel like eating, but since I haven't really eaten since the cinnamon rolls yesterday morning, I know I have to give my body some form of sustenance.

"I don't think I'm going," I say nervously.

Kaida's eyes go wide. "What do you mean? You have to go. Pride only comes around once a year. It's like Christmas for the LGBT community."

I think about my parents going to Pride to scream at those people, in particular, the teenagers. I think about them being in the group with the church and holding up signs that my mom helped make with scripture written on them in seemingly innocent penmanship and tiny, unthreatening crosses.

"I'm just not," I say a little harshly.

J.J takes a drag from their cigarette. "Are you scared?"

That's exactly what I am—scared, but not in the way they think. I'm terrified that my parents are going to see me there, and then I don't even want to think about what would happen. I'm petrified that everyone is going to find out about me and then I can no longer hold onto this secret that I've taken back for myself and packed away where it belongs. I've made my secret part of my identity, and not having that secret to hold onto terrifies me.

"No," I lie, acting like his accusation is ridiculous.

"If it's because you don't think you're allowed, you are," Kaida says. "No one cares if you're straight and go to Pride. In fact, no one even knows who's straight and who's not, you know? Even when I had a boyfriend, people just assumed I was bi. I've gone every year since I was thirteen, and it's a really fun party, honestly."

I've been staring down at my tray as she's been talking,

chewing on the side of my cheek to keep my mouth shut. I can feel the words digging into my throat, like nails sliding through the flesh dying to be released from my mouth. I'm trying to push it down, but it's not going anywhere. The words feel like a concrete block sitting in my throat. There's stomach acid touching my back teeth. J.J flicks the ash from their cigarette and I swear it's falling in slow motion.

"Yeah," they laugh. Their voice is deeper than normal and their words linger on the air. "If Kaida is accepted at Pride given how boy crazy she is, you'll be fine." Their words are too slow and I feel like they're talking to me underwater.

Nova's hand touches my arm. "Casey?" Her words drift into my ear and my own name pulls on my brain.

When I open my mouth, I go to say something along the lines of 'I'm fine' or 'I'm okay', but my brain has a different idea. "I'm gay."

6

As soon as the words leave my mouth and I look to see if I actually said that out loud, I know I did because the group's eyes are frozen on me. I never wanted to tell anyone else. I'd made that mistake before and then, I outran it. But now, no matter what I do, I can't reverse time or catch the words and shove them back down my throat. My stomach turns and I can feel the color draining from my face. My brain feels like it's being electrocuted, desperately trying to make my hands move correctly, my eyes do their thing, and the rest of my body follow suit.

I stand quickly, clumsily grabbing for my tray. "No. I…" I stand frozen in panic.

Lars's hand goes up in the air. He's been on his laptop the whole time. "Called it." His eyes don't leave the screen as he speaks and his words, like everything else, are slow and garbled.

I leave the tray on the table as I stumble away and head back toward the school building. Once I'm back inside, I practically run to the nearest bathroom, which is thankfully empty. I crash into one of the stalls and lock it behind me as if I'm being chased, but the logical part of me knows that the only thing that's chasing me is my own imaginary ghost. I fall onto my knees over the toilet and lose what little food was in my stomach. After a couple of heaves, there's nothing left, but it feels like my body wants to upchuck everything inside me, to turn me inside out.

I slowly stand using the wall of the stall when I realize there's nothing else coming up. I flush and sit on the toilet, covering my face with my hands as I sob. I just came out, again, and for the second time, I realize all those celebrities who said things would be okay, lied to me. I don't feel relieved. There was no weight lifted from my chest and I am sure as hell am not going to scream my truth to the world. On the contrary, I want to bury myself where no one will ever find me.

I don't know how much time passes. Time doesn't seem to exist right now as I visualize closing myself away into a tiny box and then putting that box inside another box, over and over. I imagine myself in the box, sealed shut with no air holes as I'm thrown into the ocean, left to sink and not drown, but suffocate. I haven't stopped sobbing as I think about the things my dad said last night and what I've heard my entire life. Everyone hates me. I disgust them. No one could ever love someone like me. My entire life, the word lesbian has always come with a disgusted look attached. It's why I've never said that word, even in my head. I'd said I was gay, but that doesn't feel right. I'm a lesbian and even the word bouncing around in my brain feels like it's dripping in something black and vile as it lingers there.

My thoughts are interrupted by the bathroom door opening. I forgot to lock it behind me as I ran in. I squelch my sobs, waiting. I hear the clunk of boots across the floor, slowly approaching.

"Casey?" It's Nova. She stops in front of the stall I'm sitting in. "Are you okay?"

"No," I say pitifully, the spit catching in my throat.

"Do you want to talk about it?"

"No," I say again, still feeling choked.

A few seconds pass and then I watch as she sits on the bathroom floor in front of the stall. "I locked the door behind me, so you're safe in here. You know you can talk to me about anything, right?"

I wipe at my eyes. "Not this."

Her arm extends awkwardly under the door and she opens her hand. After a few seconds, she huffs. "Dude, hold my hand." I take her hand. I can tell she's not comfortable in her position on the floor and after a while, she shifts. "Before I break my elbow for you, will you talk to me?"

I release her hand and watch as it disappears back underneath the door. "Okay," I exhale.

I stand slowly and take a breath before sliding the lock back and letting the door open in. The way she's looking at me, she has that curious look on her face again, but she's grinning slightly, and I feel comforted by her standing in front of me. When she smirks and raises her eyebrows, I can't control myself. I wrap my arms around her neck and bury my face in her shoulder, breathing her in as I let the darkness envelop me. A few seconds later, I realize that I probably did something inappropriate and try to separate myself from her.

"I'm sorry," I say through tears as I release her. "I know you're not a hugger."

She pulls me by my shoulders into her and wraps her arms around me. "Who the hell told you that?"

I move my arms to be around her waist. "I assumed."

"Don't assume things about me," she says against my hair.

She continues to hold me as I cry. It feels so good to be in her arms. There's nowhere else I'd rather be in the world. Even though Nova is taller than me, it feels like we're the same height when she holds me. I feel safe here like she could protect me from the words that people are going to hurl at me. I feel like she could protect me from my parents and from everyone else in my life who is going to treat me differently. In reality, I know she can't be my shield, but right now, it's nice to pretend. She doesn't even flinch when the bell rings signifying the end of lunch.

"Ignore it," she whispers in my ear when I try to let her go.

Someone tries to open the door to the bathroom and I manage to wiggle free from her hold. "We have to go," I tell her. I wipe my eyes. "I'm fine."

She looks toward the door. "Go back into the stall and count to twenty. I'll meet you in the hall." At the confused look on my face, she motions to the door. "If we walk out together, everyone is going to think we were making out in here and that'll only make things worse for you. Go."

I back myself back into the stall and listen for Nova to open the door. I know she's gone when I hear the complaints from girls as they come into the bathroom. I count to twenty, ignoring the girls talk about the latest gossip from school that I'm so detached from, I don't recognize any of the names. When I get to twenty, I open the stall slowly and wash my hands, keeping my head down. I walk past the girls and out into the hallway where Nova is waiting for me.

"You didn't have to wait on me," I tell her.

She starts walking and I follow her. "Sure I did," she says. "How else were you going to get off campus?"

I pause my walking. "What are you talking about?"

She turns around and gets close to me since the hallway is crowded. "You just came out, and from your reaction, I'm guessing you didn't mean to. It wasn't just us who heard what you said."

As the faces pass me in the hallway, they're staring at me. They've heard about the girl who came out at lunch and they're putting the pieces together that the girl was me. Some of them whisper to each other, but I can't hear what they're saying. There are kids here who go to my church. I know for a fact that Patrick does. There's no way he isn't going to hear about me, and I'd be stupid to think he wouldn't tell his parents, not to mention his aunt who's friends with my mom.

I look at Nova and I can feel the floor beneath me shift slightly as my body is begging me to go to the floor. "Where are we going?" I ask.

"The hell away from here."

She grabs my hand and there's a moment of panic I feel as people see us holding hands, but then I realize it doesn't matter now. By the end of the school day, everyone in school, and probably the entire community, is going to know about me. I hold tighter to her hand, which is the only thing keeping me from shutting down.

"We need to get to my car before the class bell rings. We can use the crowd to keep the attention off of us."

She leads me through the school, squeezing through the tight-knit packs of people who are waiting on the warning bell before they head to class. Nova and I grab our things from our lockers before she takes me out through a side door after checking that no teachers have their eyes on us. They seem to be distracted by an argument down the hall that's threatening to turn into blows.

We cross a small courtyard and she pulls me against the building as she peeks around the side. "Rent-a-cop goes on patrol during lunch, but he's headed in now. We just have to wait until he's back in his office."

"What if we get caught?"

She glances back at me, her hand still in mine. "I don't let myself get caught." She tugs on my hand as she walks semi-crouched toward the parking lot. I follow her lead and when we get to the car, she does a quick sweep with her eyes before she gestures for me to get inside. When she gets in, I don't even have time to put on my seatbelt before she guns the old car through the parking lot.

I click my seatbelt and Nova does the same once we're on the main road. Now that I'm coming off the adrenaline from ditching school, I can feel the panic rising in my chest. I lean my head back against the seat and close my eyes. "When my parents find out…" I can't finish my sentence.

"They won't find out. I've threatened the group with their lives if they say a word to anyone." She pauses for a moment. "Here." I open my eyes and she's handing her phone to me. "Text Kaida to get the word out to the school that the whole thing is a rumor."

I look down at her phone in my hand. It feels like it's made of lead, but it has the power to change everything. "But it's not a rumor. I'm a lesbian." Saying it out loud, I still don't feel relieved and even though Nova knows, there's still a moment where I'm waiting on her to say something mean or to make a disgusted face.

"I know, but if people think it's a rumor, it'll give you

some more time. If you weren't ready to come out, we can make it seem like you didn't"

I'm conflicted as I grip her phone in my hand. I don't want my parents finding out, but if people think it's a rumor, then I'm only shutting myself back into the closet. I've already done that once before and I don't think I have it in me to pack myself away again. I'm out now. I didn't mean to be, but forcing myself back in the closet is only hurting me. Even if it would be safer to lie to everyone, I'm also lying to myself, and that's not something I can do anymore. I'm not going to fly around Pride flags or anything like that any time soon, but I've been holding onto this for so long it feels like pulling teeth. Even if it means risking everything, I can't let fear rule over me anymore.

I put Nova's phone into the cupholder. "No." I think about the kid earlier in the hallway who was being bullied for being gay and how I didn't do anything for him while the other kids laughed. "It's not fair."

"It's not," she agrees. "But if you change your mind, that's okay too. You being safe is what's important, even if it doesn't feel fair."

"I know and after yesterday, I don't know if I'm safe at home."

She pulls into the parking lot of a carwash and finds a lone spot. "What happened yesterday?" She doesn't cut the engine. I don't think she's planning on leaving the car.

I explain to her what the preacher at the church said yesterday and what my dad basically regurgitated at dinner. "I was really scared that I was going to say something or do something that was going to tell them everything. There was this kid at my old church that disappeared one day. It was pretty much known amongst the youth group that he was gay, but everyone ignored it because he had never come out, or anything. We found out that he was outed by some assholes at school and his family had him sent away to be converted." I pick at my fingers. "He was gone for, like, two weeks. Then, his body came back." I exhale as I try not to picture myself hanging from the rafters as he did. "I've never been close with my parents. They've always held this power over me, so I've stayed in my place. I've always justified our relationship by saying 'well, at least they love me, even when I mess up', but I don't know if I'll be able to say that anymore. I think this is a mistake that they won't be able to forgive."

She finds my eyes as she props her elbow on the console. "You being a lesbian is not a mistake, Casey. If your parents pull that 'hate the sin, love the sinner' bullshit, or even think about sending you to one of those camps, they don't deserve to love you." Her eyes fall for a moment like she's thinking. "My grandparents threw me a coming out party last year. My grandma baked me a rainbow cake and my grandpa wears an 'I love my lesbian granddaughter' sweatshirt. That's how you should be treated, not like you're a bad person, but like you're special because you are."

I've started crying again, but these tears are softer and different from the panicked ones from before. "I didn't know you were gay," I laugh.

This makes her laugh too. "You've got to work on your gaydar, dude."

I smile, wiping my tears. "I know."

She takes my hand and her eyes return to demanding I listen. "You're going to be okay," she winks. "You've got me."

She's looking at me the way that she does sometimes like she's curious about me. My mind goes back to the night in my bedroom where I thought about kissing her as she was looking at me like this.

I carefully brush my thumb on the back of her hand. "You're my best friend, Nova."

She blinks and moves to sit back normally in her seat. "And you're one of mine." She clicks her seatbelt back and adjusts herself into a driving position. "So, we have the rest of the day to do whatever we want. We could go to my place." She considers this. "I mean, my grandparents are probably there and I know that meeting new people might be a bit much for today, but at least you can meet some people who would be happy for you."

Meeting new people wasn't exactly on my itinerary for today, especially the people who raised Nova, but then again, neither was coming out and having the entire school know that the new girl is a lesbian. It could be nice to meet adults who don't think I'm disgusting since that's what I'm used to. It could be refreshing to have someone besides Nova happy for me. Anyone who has influenced Nova must be a good person because Nova is pretty much the best person I know.

I nod, feeling slightly better. "Let's do it."

♀

Nova lives in an older brick one-story house in a community where most of the houses look like they haven't changed in decades. In fact, all the neighbors I see are older people mostly sitting on their porches or tending to some flowers in their small gardens. It's hard to believe that someone as spunky and rebellious as Nova grew up in what I could only describe as something like a retirement community.

Nova parks in the small driveway that leads to the house. "Don't be nervous. My grandparents are super chill and if anything, you'll want them to be meaner," she laughs.

"I just want them to like me."

She nudges me. "What's not to like?" I follow her up to the small front porch that has multiple plants in terra cotta pots. She unlocks the front door and I follow her into the foyer of the house. "Nan? Pops?" She calls into the house, setting her bag down. "I'm home early." I set my bag next to hers.

A woman with dark olive skin and long grey hair down to her waist rounds the corner as Nova and I go into the living room. She's wearing slouched pants and a blouse, both earth colors, and a beautiful necklace made of light-colored beads. She looks confused to see Nova, but her hazel eyes brighten when she sees me.

"Hi there." Her voice is soft and almost birdlike.

"Nova, what's going on?" A man with slightly lighter skin comes from the hallway. He has grey hair with some streaks of black still in it combed back into a thin ponytail. His eyes are almost grey.

"This is my friend, Casey," Nova tells them. "She just moved here from Arizona." I can hear in her tone that she doesn't know what she should say.

Nova's grandparents look at each other before they look at me. The woman smiles at me. "It's nice to meet you, Casey. I'm Awinita, but everyone calls me Nan." She motions to the man. "This is my husband, Onacona, but everyone calls him Pops."

"You both have beautiful names," I grin. "It's nice to meet you, too."

Nan waves at us to come with her. "Well, let's not stand here all afternoon. Come on to the kitchen, girls. I've got some bread coming out of the oven soon."

Nova offers me a grin that says 'you can breathe now' before she leads me down the hallway to their kitchen. I could smell the bread baking from the doorway and in the kitchen, it's stronger, rich and homey. Pops sits at the head of the dark wood dining table in their kitchen. Nova sits next to him opposite the kitchen and I take the seat next to hers. Nan goes into the main part of the kitchen, which is only separated from the dining area by a small counter space and cabinets above it.

Pops flicks his eyes between me and Nova. "So, what has you both out of school so early?"

"Ona," Nan warns from the kitchen. "If Nova and Casey left school, it was for a good reason." Pops winks at me, grinning. He seems sweet and the kind of older man who still thinks he's a teenager. I see what Nova loves so much about him. Nan joins us at the kitchen table sitting opposite Nova.

"Nova said you're from Arizona, Casey?" Pops asks. "You're awfully pale for a desert girl." He's teasing me, alleviating some of the nervous energy in the room.

"I am," I agree. "My parents kept me close to home." While other kids were partying in the desert and getting high off of whatever they could find, I was either at home in my room or with my friends doing nothing exciting as we were shut in one of their houses.

Nan looks at Nova before she looks back at me. "My family was from New Mexico originally, then we moved here when I was young." She looks at Pops. "Ona and I met when I was fourteen." Pops takes her small hand in his rough one.

"That's a long time," I say.

Pops smiles at Nan. "She's always been my sun." He turns his attention to me. "What are your parents like?"

I nervously flick my eyes to Nova, unsure if I should tell the truth about my parents or not. She grins and I take that to mean I'm allowed to say whatever I want. "Not like that," I tell them. "My dad rules the roost."

Nan offers a sympathetic smile. "And you don't speak much."

I'm not sure why, but I feel like I can trust Nan and Pops. It's the same trusting feeling I get when I'm around Nova. Nan and Pops feel like the loving grandparents I never had since my own are like my parents. There's something about Nan and Pops' whole demeanor like they've never been mean or judgmental toward anyone. I think hatred makes people seem older, and cold.

I hold my hands in my lap nervously, picking at my thumb. "They don't care about what I have to say."

Nova reaches over and puts her hand on top of mine beneath the table. "We do," she whispers. I believe her when she says it. I believe everything Nova says.

I rotate my hand to clasp on to Nova's hand for stability. "I came out today," I tell Nan and Pops, softly, waiting on their reaction.

They both smile at me and I can see this glint in their eyes of genuine smiles "That's exciting," Nan says. "Congratulations."

I smile back, relieved. "Thank you."

"It must not have gone as you hoped?" Pops asks.

"I didn't mean to come out." I squeeze Nova's hand gently. "Nova knew that, and she helped me."

Pop's puts his hand on Nova's shoulder, proudly. "That's our Nova." He brushes her cheek with his thumb. "Always the protector."

Nan looks at me with the same protectiveness. "When you go home, are you going to be safe?"

With one hand free, I scratch my thumb with my fingernail. There's this heaviness that comes over me that usually comes with feeling overwhelmed. "I don't know," I exhale.

"Nan, I think Casey needs a break," Nova says. "Is it okay if we go back to my room?"

I take my hand from Nova's feeling the small beads of sweat that have begun to form on the heel of my hand. The house feels warm, and I'm not sure if it's from the oven or that the air conditioning doesn't seem to be working that well, but I can feel my cheeks are flushed and worrying about my skin going pink is only making my face feel warmer.

"Of course," Nan says. She smiles at me. "Let me know if you'd like tea or anything."

I swallow, trying to keep the nervous bile from creeping up my throat. "Thank you," I stammer. "Nova's lucky to have a family like you."

Nova and I leave the kitchen and go back down the hallway to get our things. She then leads me down the other hallway to the back of the house. Her room looks exactly like I thought it would. There are homemade local band posters on the wall and a stack of CDs next to a stereo system, which is on top of her dresser. There are clothes thrown around on the floor and her covers are crumpled on her bed, unmade.

I sit on the plush carpet after tossing a t-shirt onto a small pile of laundry by the bathroom door before I cross my legs. Some of her band posters aren't what I would call age appropriate with nuns making out on one and a topless punk girl screaming into a microphone on the other. My parents would never let me have posters like this, much less even look at them.

"I like your room," I tell her.

She follows my eyes to the screaming punk girl. "I'll bet," she teases. She goes over to her stereo and starts playing a CD. A girl is half screaming, half speaking in an off tone way through the speakers. "This is her band, The Penny Loafers." Nova comes back over to where I am and kicks her boots off before sitting in front of me, cross-legged.

I slide my own shoes off and settle into the carpet. "She sounds pissed."

"Shh," Nova says, putting her finger to her lips. "Just listen."

I start packing up my things when it gets close to the time for me to leave. Nova and I sat in silence as we listened through the album she put on. Listening to a girl scream and maybe even cry about her unaccepting parents and how ugly she is to society made me feel not as alone in my current situation. Of course, I know I'm not the only teenage girl in the world going through this, but there's something different about having your own thoughts screamed back at you that makes it feel less isolating. I'd smiled as I watched Nova passionately mouth along with the lyrics 'You think my love is dirty, but with her, I feel clean.'.

Thankfully, Nova and I didn't talk much about what happened today or what I was going to do tonight since I could barely hear myself think over the music, which I think was Nova's intention. As time ticked by, however, the music started to become just noise in my head as the anxiety about facing my parents began to rise in my chest. The silence after the CD had clicked to a stop now feels uncomfortable like the silence has grown fingers and is crawling across my skin. My hands are shaking a little as I check to make sure I'd grabbed the right books from my locker as I'd been in a rush earlier.

Nova puts her hand on my arm and those cold, silent fingers from before disappear. "Are you okay?"

I don't look at her as I zip up my bag. "Fine," I try to say as even-toned as I can.

"Casey." My name is desperate in her mouth.

"Nova," I snap, gripping my bag. Immediately, I hang my head, blinking back tears. "I'm sorry."

"Don't be sorry. You're scared. I get it."

"You really don't," I say as I sling my bag over my shoulder. "You were welcomed with open arms when you came out. I'll be lucky if I'm still allowed to sleep in my own bed tonight."

She grabs her wallet and keys from her bag. "You're right. I don't know what it's like to not be accepted by my family. But, I do know what it's like to be scared that you won't be accepted by everybody else. That fear is pretty universal, I think." She nods to her poster. "Penny wrote that entire album when she was nineteen. She had left home at sixteen and three years later, she was still feeling the pain of not being accepted."

"So, it doesn't get better?"

Nova sighs. "I don't think people really change, but I think you will get better. I think as we get older, we'll get tougher, and our bullshit meter will widen, so certain things won't matter like they do now."

I flick my eyes back to the poster. "Are you telling me to run away like she did?"

"No," she says softly. "I'm saying that you don't have to have it all figured out at sixteen. I'm saying you're allowed to be pissed and you're allowed to carry that pain with you. People think once you come out, things suddenly brighten and the world seems alright again, but that's not true. In some ways, it gets harder." She touches my arm. "I'm telling you that you don't need permission to feel what you feel. You might always be angry, and that's okay."

I exhale and look down at my feet. "I want to press fast forward through the bad parts. I want to skip ahead to the part where I'm living with my partner in our studio apartment and, I don't know, have a cat, or something."

Nova smiles. "Nan would say you have to live through the bad parts first, but I won't. I'll tell you what Penny would say."

I glance up at her. "Which is?"

"Fuck 'em," she shrugs. "Don't live your life for other people. You get that studio apartment with the girl you love and if you want a cat, get a damn cat. You're allowed to be selfish and want everything. You just gotta hold your middle fingers up high and not take shit from anyone."

Her pep talk has made a little bit of my anxiety go away and her passion has made me smile. "I don't know if I could do this without you."

Her lip ring hits her teeth when she momentarily bites her lip. "I'm not going anywhere."

In the living room, Nan stops us. "Headed off already?"

I wish I could stay here in this safe bubble for a little bit longer. I'd feel better if I could be around people who accept me, but at some point I have to go home and I know that's it's better for me to go now while I still have time to beat the bus to my street than to be in more trouble than I already am.

"I'm sure my parents have heard from the school by now," I tell Nan. "It's better to face them now than to wait and make things worse."

She holds the tops of my arms. "You're welcome here anytime, Casey."

"Thank you," I grin.

"Don't be a stranger," Pops says behind Nan. "We're old. We could use the company," he smiles.

"She'll be back," Nova tells them. "Count on it."

7

Nova pulls to the curb in her usual spot by my house. We didn't talk much as she drove. I wasn't sure what to even say, apart from talking about how afraid I am, which I'm sure she's tired of hearing. I'd tried to put myself in the future, imagining the studio apartment and the cute fluffy cat running around. I'd tried to imagine what it would be like to come home to the girl I love. I didn't picture a person, but more of a feeling like being wrapped in a warm blanket. I didn't imagine her as anyone in particular, but little things popped into my head like a warm laugh and the sound of boots on the floor and lips with a black lip ring pressed to my cheek.

It isn't until Nova puts the car in 'park' that I'm jolted out of my head. "What are you doing?" I ask.

She has her elbow resting on the door and she has the side of her head against her palm. The other hand is wrapped around the steering wheel. "Waiting," she says like it's the most obvious thing in the world.

"You don't have to wait. I'll be okay."

She doesn't move, making a point. "I don't doubt you'll be okay. You're a badass." She winks. "But, I'll be here just in case."

As I walk toward my house, I can feel the anxiety radiate through my chest. It's making my entire body hurt as it circles around my arms and crawls up the back of my neck. I can feel those cold fingers from before, but they're not silent anymore. They're loud, scraping noises that accompany the voice in my head telling me to turn back. The voice seems to be shoving me by my chest to run back to Nova, then keep running until she and I are so far away that no one knows who we are. I want to feel the way I did earlier with her when her arms were around me—safe. I want to curl myself up so tightly that I could fit in the spaces between her ribcage, living like a bird right next to her heart.

I slowly open my front door and linger in the foyer after putting my bag by the staircase, waiting to hear if anyone is home. There's a hope I've let grow inside of me that Mom has been gone all day running errands and that maybe, just maybe, no one has called her, so this afternoon is going to be like any other.

"Casey?" My mom's voice echoes through the house from the dining room. "Come here." I don't know if her tone is off or if it's in my head, but the way she sounds, something is wrong.

I expected my mom to be at the dining room perched behind her laptop like she always is. What I didn't expect, however, was to see her sans laptop sitting next to my dad, who isn't supposed to be home for a couple more hours. He has this look on his face that says whatever has brought him home early is not only an inconvenience but something personal. There's also an intensity behind his eyes that doesn't make me feel safe and I know if I turn right now, I could probably be down the street before he could get to the front door.

"Sit down," he orders, making me jump.

I know he knows and I can feel the tightness build in my lungs, the fingers squeezing the air out of me as I sit across from them. I feel transparent except for my face, which has the word 'lesbian' written across it in thick black paint. My skin prickles with a feeling of panic and I force the air in and out of my lungs through my nose.

Mom has her hands in her lap and she's sitting so stiffly that I half expect the world to be frozen. "I received an interesting phone call today," she says with an even tone.

The best thing I can do right now is to not dig a hole to bury myself in. "Oh?" I pretend to be ignorant instead.

Neither of them is buying my ignorance. "You were absent from your last few classes," Mom says. "You had a quiz in history that you didn't take."

She knows how studious I am and that I don't do well mentally if I don't do well on a quiz. She knows that failure isn't an option for me. I try to keep my breathing even, not giving her the satisfaction of seeing the gears turning in my head thinking of how I'm going to make that quiz up.

Dad's eyes are like daggers on my face. "Where did you go?"

I can't involve Nova or her grandparents in this. My parents would find them in the phonebook and I don't want Nan or Pops to be on the receiving end of my Mom's passive aggressive nature. My parents can't know that Nova got me out of school, either. They can't know about her at all. They have to think I left school on my own, completely alone. I quickly scramble my brain to remember the layout of the town.

"I wasn't feeling well." I keep my voice low. "So, I walked to the park to get some fresh air."

I can see the muscles in Dad's jaw tighten. "You thought you could leave school without permission?"

I can't look at them anymore. I trace the pattern of the swirls in the wood of our dining room table instead. "I wasn't thinking, I guess."

Dad scoffs. "I knew that ghetto school was a bad idea. How did a student manage to walk through the front doors without anyone noticing?" His question is rhetorical, so I don't answer. "You're too smart to do something so stupid, Casey."

"How did you get home?" Mom asks.

"I walked," I say quickly.

Dad's eyes are no less intense and I can feel them burning through me. "I had to leave an important meeting to be here," he says through his teeth. "Do you want me to lose my job, Casey?"

I pick at my fingers in my lap feeling slightly relieved that this is the worst thing they're going to yell at me about today. They don't know about what happened at school. I start to wonder if the rumor fizzled before it could get too far down the grapevine.

"I'm sorry." I try to sound convincing, but I can feel the smile on my lips, feeling the weight lift from my chest.

"Joyce called me," Mom says. When she says her name, I feel like I've been punched in the back. I knew Patrick would tell her. "Is there anything else you want to tell us, Casey?"

The way Dad is looking at her, Mom didn't tell him what Joyce told her on the phone. He doesn't know, but she does. I never thought she would be on my side with something like this, but I'd hoped, anyway. Dad was the one I was most worried about, but I can tell that thinking I could trust her, even just a little, was the wrong thing to do. I shouldn't have let my guard down.

"What did Joyce say?" Dad asks her.

"I think it's best if your daughter tells you the secret she's been keeping from us," Mom says.

I feel trapped like I'm glued to my chair. My mouth is dry and my throat feels like there are razor blades in it. I'm glancing between them, regretting getting out of Nova's car this afternoon. I should have listened to the voice in my head that told me to run, but I stupidly let myself believe that there was a chance they didn't know anything. I consider lying to them and telling them that it's just a rumor like Nova suggested earlier, but I know they won't believe me. I can tell by how Mom is looking at me that she wouldn't believe me, anyway. She knows she's caught me and there's no escape.

Dad's expression is unchanging and I fear he's going to crack his teeth. "Casey Hope Walker, you know secrets are the same as lies, and lying is a sin."

If I don't tell him the truth, Mom is going to and I can already hear the tone she's going to use when she does. She has this specific way of speaking about things she hates like her words are a viscous liquid dripping between her teeth. It's how she talked about certain women back at our old church, the women who were secret alcoholics or those who had gotten a divorce.

I look down at my hands in my lap. "I'm gay," I say in a

low tone.

When I look back up a second later, I can tell Dad isn't comprehending what I said.   "What did you just say?" His voice is low and threatening.

Before I can say it again, Mom jumps in. "Our daughter is a lesbian, Dalton."

She's using the exact disgusted tone I knew she would. She says 'lesbian' the same way I've heard her say 'black' or 'foreign', like words she believes shouldn't be said too loud in public. I can see the disgust on her face, like the way most people look at fresh roadkill like someone should get rid of it before it starts to smell.

The way Dad is looking at me reminds me of the way the ocean gets all calm and eerily serene before it pulls back and floods entire cities. "Is that true?"

My eyebrows pull together and I grip the sides of my chair afraid that my dad has one of those switches beneath his feet that's going to open up a secret door placed just under my chair and I'm going to be dropped down into a basement that doesn't exist, never to be seen or heard from again.

"Yes," I choke out around the tightness in my throat.

His eyes are fixed in a cold stare. "No." He says it like I had been asking permission. A simple word, but it feels like a sharp crack in a window. I can feel the explosion coming on. I can see it in his shaking hands and his twitching lip. "Absolutely not. My daughter will not be one of those people." He's saying it to me like simply shaming me is going to change my mind.

Mom's lip is curled in the same way Dad's is. "Patrick mentioned a girl, a brown girl." She emphasizes 'brown' like she's holding back a gag. "Have you had sex with her?" If her face was any more twisted, she wouldn't look human.

I can't keep Nova a secret anymore. I don't know if Patrick mentioned her by name, and I'm not going to ask. I can only hope that by talking about her, I can make her seem like someone they'd approve of, despite her skin tone.

"She's just my friend," I say confidently, so maybe they'll

believe me. "She's pretty much my only friend."

Dad stands abruptly from the table and leans toward me with his palms on the table. "I won't allow that kind of sin in my house." He hasn't heard a word I've said. "Either you choose right now to get right with God, or you can leave this house."

"It's not a choice," I tell them. I have nothing to lose at this point and I decide to fight back as Nova would. "This is who I am. I can't choose to be straight just like you can't choose to be gay."

Dad grabs the top of my arm from across the table. "God can take any sin, Casey. You can choose not to act on this sin and pray to God for him to take it away. You can choose to do the right thing and be with a boy. You'll get married and have children and forget all about this sin that has tempted you." When he releases my arm, he shoves me back a little in my seat before taking his own.

I'm angry that my mom let him grab me like that and did nothing about it. She only sat there and nodded along with everything he said. "Is it this girl at school who has tempted you, Casey?" Mom asks.

I'm trying to hold back tears and I haven't really been able to breathe since I sat down, but the breaths are coming ragged now not giving my lungs a choice but to work beyond the panic.

"No." I'm desperate for them to listen. "No one is tempting me. I've known who I am for a couple of years now."

Mom shakes her head. "You're going to pray away this sin and I'm going to find you a nice boy in the church, like Patrick."

I don't know why I thought this conversation was going to go any differently, but there's a part of me that wants to instigate them. I want to scream my truth and face the consequences no matter what they are. It's what Nova would do. She'd told me to lift my middle fingers and be unapologetic. Penny would let love be louder and in my head, there's a mix of both attitudes.

"No," I say defiantly. "I'm going to fall in love with a girl and there's nothing you can do about it. You can't pray something like this away because to get rid of this would be getting rid of me. I won't be with a boy. I don't like boys."

They both look at me like I'm the devil sitting in front of them. They don't see me as their daughter anymore. I can practically see the love they once had from me leave their cold hearts. A part of me, a big part, knew this would happen. I knew it would go down like this, and I still let myself think that maybe they'd see past that bigotry and love me for me, but I should've never believed it. I should've listened to my instincts.

Dad points to the door. "Get out." His voice is shaking like his hand.

I look to Mom to come to my defense. I don't expect her to accept me, or even love me anymore, but I can't imagine she'd kick out her only child. "Listen to your father, Casey," she says, no longer looking at me.

I look between them, tears filling my eyes. "Forever?" It sounds so pitiful in my throat and I feel like a child for asking.

"Until you have come back to God, you won't step foot in this house," Dad says.

I look at Mom. "Where am I supposed to go?" The tears have escaped my eyes now. "Do you expect me to live on the street?"

I can see a little bit of falter on her face. "Dalton, if we make her leave, she'll go to the girl who tempted her in the first place."

Dad lowers his finger, but he doesn't change his mind. "I won't have someone like her in my house."

I'm sobbing now. "How can you do this to me? I'm your only child. Do you not love me anymore?"

I hate the way they're looking at me. In their eyes, I'm some random person they're preaching to on the street. I'm one of those 'sinners' they wave their sign at, practically beating them over the head in the process.

"You can be forgiven of this sin, Casey," Mom says, her voice back to normal. "All you have to do is pray and God will bring you back home and back into the life He wants for you."

I hate them. I don't care if they love me anymore because I don't love them. Parents are supposed to love their kids no matter what. Parents love is supposed to be unconditional, even if the kid does something the parents don't agree with. I've seen parents stick by their kids for murder and mine can't even stand by me for love. My parents don't deserve to call themselves parents. A dark thought comes into my mind that I'm glad my mom had a stillborn baby and those miscarriages because she didn't deserve to have more children. She didn't deserve me. I don't want to be around them any more than they want to be around me.

I wipe my eyes and stand quickly, knocking the chair over behind me. "I hate you," I yell as I storm off toward the stairs.

Dad is loudly quoting the fifth commandment—honor thy father and mother. Mom is yelling for me to come back to the dining room, but for the first time in my life, I don't do as I'm told. I grab my book bag and practically jog up the stairs and to my bedroom where I pack as much as I can into it. I don't know where I'm going, but I'm not wanted here. My parents don't love me or care what happens to me, so why should I? Maybe I can find a shelter to stay in, or maybe it's warm enough that I could find a nice park bench. I'd sleep under a bridge if it meant being away from them.

My parents are still yelling for me downstairs, but I don't plan on leaving that way. With everything I need in my book bag, I throw open my window. I toss down my book bag since there's nothing breakable inside before I climb through my window, then shut it behind me. I shuffle across the roof and slide down the side just like I did the night of the show. That night feels so long ago now. Once my feet hit the ground, I grab my bag and run down the sidewalk despite the lingering heat in the late afternoon sun. I don't know if Nova has left by now. I wouldn't blame her if she did.

I slow when I get over the hill and I see Nova still sitting in her car on the side of the road. I could fall to the ground in relief to see her. She's looking down at her phone, so she doesn't see me yet. As I approach her car, I can feel the tears coming back into my eyes along with the fear that has come back to my spine, clenching its cold fingers around my muscles. She looks up when I open the door. I put my book bag in between my legs. I shut the door and freeze, unsure of what to do now.

Nova looks at my stuffed book bag in the floor. "I see that went as well as expected," she says sarcastically.

I slide down in the seat, defeated. "I knew this was going to happen." The guilt sits in the bottom of my stomach, burning. "I should've kept my mouth shut. Why didn't I lie? It would've been so much easier to lie."

Her hand is soft on my arm. "If I pushed you, I'm sorry. I never meant for this to happen." "You didn't," I assure her. "I opened my mouth first. I did this to myself. I've screwed up my entire life, and for what? My parents didn't change their minds. I didn't make them realize anything. All I did was hurt myself."

Her thumb moves in tiny circles across my wrist, comforting me. "Not that this is going to help right now, but I'm proud of you. I mean, the rest sucks, but you stood up for yourself. I told you, you're a badass."

"You're right," I sigh. "The rest sucks." I move to sit up straighter and she takes her hand away. "I feel selfish for needing you."

She side-eyes me. "It's okay to need someone." She clicks her seatbelt back on. "What do you need?"

I click my seatbelt too. "Can we just go somewhere? I don't want to be this close to my house anymore." A thought pops into my head. "Are there any shows tonight?"

She's surprised by my suggestion. "There's always a show somewhere. Did you like it that much last time?"

I couldn't really think while the music was going and that's what I want right now. "I want to be somewhere that's louder than my brain."

She nods, considering this. "I feel that."

The shirt I have on right now, one of my standard blouses with a collar that hugs my throat, feels like it's choking me right now. When I look at it, all I can think about is being around my parents and their voices in my head as I was growing up yelling at me when I'd want to wear what the other girls did. If I dared to buy myself anything revealing, I'd be called a 'whore', or that I was 'asking for the wrong attention'. I don't want the blouse on anymore.

I look back at the clothes in Nova's backseat. "This might sound weird, but do you have anything I could wear that isn't this?" I gesture to my top.

She looks me over. "I like that top on you." Then: "Okay, one second." She reaches into the back seat, then offers me what looks like a guy's dark grey/green t-shirt. "Don't worry, it's mine."

I unlatch my seatbelt and pull my shirt to my bellybutton. Nova goes back to digging through the pile of clothes in her backseat and I take my shirt off the rest of the way. I slip the t-shirt over me and I know it's long on me, so I tuck the hem into the waistband of my jeans before rolling the sleeves, since those are long too.

Nova hands me a flannel. "Trust me. The place we're going has AC that works in overtime." I hesitantly take the checkered flannel from her. "That's mine, too," she grins.

I slip Nova's flannel over my arms and start to button the top buttons. She reaches over and lightly smacks my hands away. "It's not a church, Saint Casey," she laughs, undoing the few buttons I'd done up.

I move my eyes away from her and calm my thudding heart that's focused on Nova's clothes on my body. "What are the odds of you ever wearing one of my tops?" I laugh to myself.

Her eyes flicking up to mine makes me look at her again. She brushes my blonde hair back from my shoulders. "I'll wear one of your blouses the day you get something on your face pierced."

I brush the tip of my finger against the ring sat in the

middle of her lip. "Like yours?"

She smiles and sits back in her seat normally. "We can't both have the same thing. I have my doubts that you'd get a needle in your skin, though."

Her teasing me makes me smile. "And what makes you think that?"

She shrugs and puts the car in 'drive'. "I'm assuming you don't have a very high pain tolerance."

I copy her shrug. "Don't assume things about me."

She smirks at her own words coming from my mouth. "Fair enough."

♀

I'm not entirely sure how, but when we get to the venue after stuffing our faces with fried onion rings and milkshakes at a fast food place, Nova is able to walk straight past the security guy at the door without more than a casual nod. She grabs my hand when we get inside and leads me through the crowd until she finds a spot that she likes. When the band comes on, the crowd erupts. Unlike the last show, the lead singer doesn't say much before the music starts. This environment is exactly what I needed after everything that happened today. I feel my screams in the throat of the lead singer and her rage radiates in my chest. It seems like this day has dragged on for a week and I haven't been able to really breathe. I'm breathing now, though, as I jump along with the rest of the crowd and let my hair swing in whatever way it wants. Nova still has my hand and we raise our arms in the air as we sway and jump, letting the music move us. I'm safe here with Nova. No one can find me. No one can see me. It's just me and Nova in this crowd, and the music belongs to us.

After the show, Nova and I leave with the rest of the crowd out of the front entrance. When we pass the security guard, Nova waves at him. "See you later, Mo." The guy who must be Mo waves back as he's in conversation with one of the bartenders.

Nova and I continue to be in the wave of the crowd that breaks apart in the parking lot. "You know him?" I ask her when we get into the car.

She turns the engine over and I'm thankful for the AC that comes out. The venue was cold at first, but it quickly warmed up as everyone filled in the spaces and moved around. "Mo was a friend of my dad's. He's how I know what shows are going on around the city."

I shrug the shoulders of the flannel off of me so the shirt falls to the crooks of my elbows and the AC hits my bare upper arms. "Have you ever talked to him about your dad?"

"When I was younger, I did. Mo only knew my dad at work, though. He told me my dad wasn't the type to talk about personal stuff."

I move my hair to the side to relieve the back of my neck. "So, that's where you get it from."

She nudges me. "I tell you stuff."

I teasingly roll my eyes. "You never talk about what's going on in your head. Getting you to talk about your feelings and stuff is like pulling teeth."

Her eyes look into mine. "And what about you, Casey?" She's being her usual sarcastic self, talking to me like a psychiatrist. "What are you feeling right now?"

I cross my arms over my chest. "I know you're deflecting, but seeing as I overshare, I'm going to answer you anyway." I sit back. "I feel lost, but also not. I feel this longing to be accepted by my parents, but I also don't care if they accept me." I tap my forehead. "It's all very weird in here right now."

The parking lot has mostly cleared out by now and Nova starts driving through it. She glances at me and smiles. "You're a real weirdo, you know that?"

I smile too. "You're the one who keeps wanting to be around me, so what does that say about you?"

"It says I'm just as weird as you are," she smirks.

8

I linger by the front door of Nova's house with my book bag as she steps in. She turns toward me and her eyebrows push together. "What are you doing?"

I nod into the house. "I'll wait while you ask. I don't want to intrude."

I can tell Nova is getting ready to say something along the lines of 'that's ridiculous', but then Nan appears in the foyer behind Nova. "I thought I heard you come in," she says, laying her hand on Nova's shoulder. She looks at the door and eyes me the same way Nova did. "Casey, sweetheart, why are you outside?" I don't have to say anything. She already knows. She releases Nova's shoulder and beckons me inside. "Come on."

I step through the foyer and Nova takes my book bag from me. Pops is in the living room and with one look from Nan, he nods. "Make yourself at home, Casey."

"If I had somewhere else to go, I swear I would get out of your hair," I tell them. "I'm sure I can find somewhere by tomorrow. I think there are some teen shelters in the city."

"Is there something wrong with us?" Pops asks. He's smiling and I know he's teasing me.

"No," I stammer. "It's just sudden and…"

Nan rubs the top of my arm. "You stay here as long as you want. Go on to Nova's room. I'll heat y'all up something to eat."

"Thank you." A wave of relief washes over me, knowing that at least for tonight, I have somewhere to feel safe.

Nova stays in the living room as I go back to her room. I set my bag down and notice the folded blanket sat on top of a pillow that's the case doesn't match the rest of Nova's bed. I go into the attached bathroom and see a white and pink toothbrush sat on the side of the sink with my name written in permanent marker on the handle.

Nova comes into her room a few minutes later as I'm sat on the side of the bed and gestures to my bag at the end of the bed. "You're not unpacked?"

"I wasn't sure if I should. My parents could change their minds, or Nan and Pops could decide that they don't want another mouth to feed." My thumb is raw and I wince. "You could decide you don't want me around anymore. I didn't want to get comfortable yet."

She sits next to me on the bed and takes my hand away from my mouth. "I know this might be a hard concept for you to wrap your head around, but there are people who care about you." She bumps my shoulder with hers. "Especially me. You're one of my best friends, and you can ask Kaida or J.J, or even Lars. To me, my friends are family." She puts her arm around my shoulders. "My grandparents weren't just being polite when they said you could stay as long as you wanted. They meant it, and they never say things they don't mean."

"I noticed the toothbrush that was waiting on me," I laugh.

She laughs too. "Nan has that intuition in her." She stops smiling. "As far as your parents, I don't think they'll change their minds. Not all parents understand how rad it is to have a kid who's different. Some people are just assholes and having a spawn doesn't make them better people. It's easy to have a kid, but accepting a kid for who they are is different."

Nova is my best friend and even though I have feelings for her to the point that being anywhere close to her makes me feel like I'm going to explode, I would be okay if she only wanted to be my friend. "I guess I should unpack."

She goes to her dresser across the room. "I'll move some of my stuff over. There's extra room in my closet too if you need it."

I take my things over to the drawer and fold the clothes

that I had tossed into the bag before I put them in the drawer next to her things. There's no mistaking our clothes. Her clothes are mostly black with occasional dark earth tones. My clothes are mostly white with occasional yellow and pink. I hang up a few blouses in Nova's closet next to her jackets and flannels, then take the rest of my toiletries to the bathroom.

When I go back out to her room, she's kicked her boots off and is sat on her bed slouched over her phone. She glances up at me. "Sit. You look as stiff as a damn board." I kick off my own shoes and sit next to her on the bed. "Kaida wants an update."

I grab my own phone from Nova's side table. "She hasn't texted me."

Nova smiles and I notice her eyes are looking at my screen. "You have that picture of us as your wallpaper." I can feel myself start to blush. She turns her phone toward me. Her wallpaper is the same photo. "It's a good picture."

I put my phone down on the bed. "I guess the group should know what's going on."

She nods as she starts typing. "Do you want to read it before I send it? I don't want to say something you're not comfortable with."

"I trust you." I stand from the bed and go over to the dresser. "I'm going to shower to get the grossness from the show off of me." I grab underwear and pajamas.

She gestures toward the bathroom. "Towels are in the little closet."

I tie my hair up into a messy bun on the top of my head so my hair doesn't get wet and I quickly wash my body using the soap Nova uses, a woodsy smelling soap that has a slight floral smell underneath it. I get out a few minutes later and dress in pajamas.

Nova looks up from where she's still sitting on the bed on her phone when I walk out of the bathroom. "Nan has dinner warmed for us. Are you hungry?"

Even though Nova and I stopped for a snack before the show, I still feel like there's nothing left in my stomach. "Starving, actually."

As Nova walks by me, she pokes my hair, which is still sat on top of my head. "Cute," she says as she opens the door and starts down the hallway.

Nova and I go back to her room once we're finished with our late dinner. We sat at the table for a while talking to Nan and Pops. It was so different from dinner with my parents. We were all laughing and there was this look of love and warmth on their faces as they looked at each other. Pops even reached over and plucked a green bean from Nova's bowl, which made me laugh because he pretended he didn't do it.

Nan and Pops have gone off to their bedroom for the night, so the house is quiet. Nova informs me that she's going to shower since she still has dried sweat on her back from the show. I grab a book from my book bag and sit on her bed while I wait for her. I hear her singing in the shower. I recognize the lyrics from the show earlier, but Nova's voice is softer and the song sounds a lot different—better, in my opinion. A few minutes later, she comes out of the bathroom in plaid pajama pants and a plain t-shirt. Her hair is damp and she runs a hand through it as she sits on the bed next to me.

She leans over my shoulder. "What are you reading?"

I continue to look down at the pages, trying to ignore how good she smells. "Ocean acidity and how humans are killing the coral reefs."

I glance at her and see the smirk on her lips. "Nerd."

I turn my head and our noses are nearly touching. "Punk," I tease. I didn't realize how close she was to me. I turn my head back toward the book and lay it on her side table.

"Are you tired?"

"A little," I shrug. "I think my body is, but my brain is wired."

She climbs behind me on the bed and rests her back against the wall. Her legs are on either side of my hips. "Nan used to braid my hair in the evenings when I was little. It's the only thing that would make me sleepy. I was kind of wild as a kid."

"Just as a kid?" I laugh.

She puts her hands softly on my shoulders as she laughs too. "So, what do you say?"

"That sounds nice."

She carefully takes my hair down from the bun and puts my elastic on her wrist. She brushes through my hair with her fingers, her short nails scratching my scalp softly. "I'm sorry your life is kind of falling apart."

I sigh, letting my eyes relax. "Yeah, me too." I thought things were okay, but having to come out felt like a bomb went off in my family. All the pieces I thought were fitting together just scattered all over the place.

She starts loosely braiding my hair. "Were things better before you came here?"

"No." I place my hand on her shin, feeling the flannel material of her pajama pants. "Things were always kind of tense like I was waiting for the thing that was going to destroy us." My finger brushes her ankle. "You're the only part of my life that's good right now."

Her fingers brush the top of my back as she works. She's silent for a few seconds. "I'm sorry."

"I'm not," I smile. I feel her fingers go down my back and I think I've said too much. "You have a pretty singing voice."

Her fingers pause for a moment. "You heard that, huh?"

I've taken my hand away from her leg and I have the side of my thumb between my teeth. "Yeah. I like it, though."

Her hand reaches around me and she lowers my arm back down to her leg. I start playing with the hem of her pant leg again. Her hands continue on my hair. "Thank you. I had that song from earlier stuck in my head and the only way to get it out is to sing it if that makes sense."

"It does. My mom does the same thing with hymns. Well, she used to, I mean. She hasn't sung in a long time. I think she's been too sad to sing."

Nova runs her fingers through my hair undoing the braid. "It sounds like you were raised by some pretty miserable people."

"Yeah, I guess so." I feel the guilt creep back into my stomach at the mention of my mom. "Can I tell you something? You have to promise you won't judge me."

She's playing with the ends of my hair. "I promise."

"Earlier, when my parents were yelling at me about coming back to God and stuff, I started thinking that I was glad my mom had to suffer birthing a dead baby and having those miscarriages. I thought she didn't deserve more children if she was going to treat me like that." I exhale. "That's messed up, isn't it?"

Her hands move to my shoulders and she massages them gently. "No. I think it says a lot that you didn't say it out loud because you totally could have. I probably would've said something that harsh if someone was telling me I wasn't allowed to be myself."

"I couldn't. I'm angry and I even told them I hated them, but I don't think to say my mom deserved what happened to her is something I could take back."

Nova puts her chin on my shoulder. "You don't have to justify yourself. The guilt you're feeling is them getting inside your head. Your parents are assholes and they probably always will be. Stop letting them be the voices in your head."

I lean my head on hers. "I don't know what I'd do without you, Nova."

She exhales a laugh. "Probably still be in the closet."

"Maybe," I sigh. I feel her hand by my hip where my shirt has ridden up and goosebumps raise on my skin. I shift and when she lifts her head, I get off the bed. "I need to brush my teeth," I tell her and walk to the bathroom.

I take a few breaths behind the closed door, calming the feeling under my skin. When Nova touches me, it feels like a drink of water after being dehydrated and climbing into bed after a stressful day all wrapped into one feeling. I want her to touch me in ways that I've never been touched before. I don't know if I should allow myself to think of Nova in that way. After everything she's done for me, I don't know what I would do if I screwed everything up.

After I brush my teeth, I open the door to see Nova right outside, leaning against the door frame. My glittery blonde hair tie is still around her wrist, but I don't mention it. She grins at me. "Left."

I've been concentrating on the ring in her lip. "What?"

She motions toward her bed. "I sleep on the left if that's okay with you."

I nod and squeeze by her. "Yeah, of course. I'm not picky."

I hear the bathroom door close and I go toward the bed. I grab the extra pillow Nan sat out for me and crawl into Nova's bed, getting comfortable on the right side, which is against the wall. The extra blanket is folded at the feet, but I don't think I'll need it. A few minutes later, Nova flips the light off and I feel her crawl in next to me, since I'm faced toward the wall.

I can feel her shoulder against my back. "Comfortable enough?"

I close my eyes, feeling sleep take me over. "Hair braiding works," I mumble.

"Every time," she laughs. "Goodnight."

9

I open my eyes slightly and realize that it's morning. I'm still faced toward the wall, but I can feel that the bed is empty beside me. I flip over slowly, letting my eyes adjust. Nova is dressed and fastening her belt. I watch her as she puts her vest over her shoulders and grabs her boots.

She glances at the bed. "Hey," she says softly. "Did you sleep okay?"

"Like the dead," I groan. "I don't even remember dreaming."

"Probably for the best." She adjusts her shirt. "Do you want coffee?"

I move from the bed and go to the dresser. "Sure, thanks." I start to get my clothes from the dresser.

"Are you nervous?"

The side of my thumb is back in my mouth. "What is this, twenty questions?" I joke. "Of course I am."

She gently lowers my arm and takes my hand. "You know I've got you, right? Anyone says shit, I'll knock their lights out."

I pump her hand before letting go. "I know. I don't mind if they say things, though. Don't get in trouble for me."

She frowns. "No promises."

I close the dresser drawer and face her with my clothes pressed to my chest. "Do you think I'm weak?"

Her brows push together. "Weak? Hell no." She touches my elbow. "Do you know how rare it is for someone to keep a soft heart in this world?" Her fingers brush my arm. "You're a rarity, Casey Walker. A beautiful, soft rarity."

I feel the blush crossing my cheeks and I start to walk

past her, knowing that if she touches me any longer, I'm going to say or do something I shouldn't. "I'll be out soon," I say as I close the bathroom door behind me.

Once I shower, dry my hair, and get dressed, I go out into the kitchen where everyone else is. Nan smiles at me and hands me a plate with a potato hash on it. "Good morning, Casey. Did you sleep okay?"

I nod. "I did. Thank you." I sit in the seat next to Nova. I see that there's a cup of coffee in front of me.

Nova grins. "I wasn't sure if you took milk and sugar."

I pick up the coffee cup. "No, this is perfect. Thank you." I sip the warm coffee, which helps me feel more awake already.

Pops smiles at me as he forks his own breakfast. "I knew I liked you."

Nan joins us at the kitchen table with her own breakfast of oats and fruit. She sips her tea. "If you girls don't want to go to school today, we won't make you. You had a hard day yesterday, Casey."

I glance at Nova before I smile at Nan. "I appreciate it, but the school will call my parents if I'm out. Besides, we have a quiz in English that we can't miss."

"We do?" Nova asks. "Shit, I forgot."

"Language," Nan scolds.

Nova and I are in her car heading to school when she turns the music down and glances over to me. "You know I like you the way you are, right?"

I furrow my brow to cover the blush in my cheeks. "What are you talking about?"

"Earlier, you asked me if you were weak, but being soft isn't being weak. I like that you're soft and forgiving." She tugs at my shirt. "I like your blouses and that you care about jellyfish, even though they're brainless. It's refreshing to know someone who hasn't allowed themselves to harden because the world has told them to." She releases the hem of my shirt. "Don't change who you are just because some assholes don't approve."

I look her over. "And what about you? Is this who you really are?"

She smirks. "Hell yeah. I've always been a bit rebellious and a little bit of a troublemaker. I like to challenge the status quo, I guess. Nothing makes me happier than to see some conservative asshole squirm."

I play with my thumbnail. "I wish I could be like that. I feel like I'm so boring."

She gives me a look. "Are you kidding? Who you are as a person is rebelling against the norm. Believe me, the minute you kiss a girl in public, you'll definitely make people squirm."

I blush, thinking about kissing a girl. "I guess so."

She grins. "And you're not boring by any means. Wanting to lay low and do your own thing isn't boring. I know that I get a little passionate, but I don't expect you to be like that, too." Her hand taps my arm. "Someone has to keep me grounded."

In English, Nova absentmindedly plays with my hair tie, which is still around her wrist. I can't help but bite my lip as to not smile as I watch her out of the corner of my eye. There's something so cute about how my glittery blonde hair tie sticks out from the rest of her dark clothes. Sleeping next to her last night had been comforting. I didn't know sleeping next to someone could feel like that. I was exhausted last night, but there was a part of me that didn't want to sleep because I didn't trust that in my sleep I wouldn't try to cuddle up to her and be closer than I was supposed to be.

I can feel eyes on me as Nova and I walk the halls, but no one dares to say anything because Nova has this look on her face like she'll beat the crap out of anyone who does. Even at lunch, I can see the way she looks at her friends. She's not angry with them, but she's watching them like she's afraid they're going to say something they shouldn't.

J.J has an unlit cigarette dangling between their lips. "Now that we know you're a giant lesbian, you can go to Pride with us."

Nova nearly calls him out, but I stop her with a hand on her arm under the table for a moment. "My parents will be there," I tell J.J nervously.

"So, we'll sneak you in," Kaida says. "You can borrow some of my clothes and I have a wig you can borrow, too. They'll never know it's you." From her tone, I can tell that she's brought this idea up to Nova before now, or the two of them have come up with it together, and her eyes flick towards Nova for approval.

"Plus, the extremists don't march or anything," Nova says carefully. "They're kept herded behind a barrier. If we avoid that section, we'll be fine." She grins at me. "That's if you want to go. We'll do what you want, at your pace."

Nova and her friends have been attending Pride together every year since they became friends. I don't know if Nova would still go if I didn't, but I hope she would. Still, I don't want to make her make that decision. Plus, I want to go. I want to see people like me and I want to see what my life could be like, minus the rejection and the fear. The thought of seeing two girls kiss makes my stomach flutter.

I smile at Nova. "Yeah, let's go."

♀

It's been a few days since I've come out, and that I've been staying at Nova's place. There have been passive comments at school, but nothing I can't handle. No one dares say anything about me when Nova's around. I haven't heard from my parents, and each day that passes, I have this lingering anxiety that I shouldn't get too comfortable where I am. Each time I hear a car pass the house, there's a moment where I think it's going to be my parents or someone from a conversion camp coming to pick me up. I don't let this fear show on my face, but I know Nova knows something is up when I freeze in the middle of our conversations.

But, with that fear and paranoia comes something else,

too. I get to see Nova be who she is both at school and when she's around her grandparents. She's mostly the same wherever she is, but she has this gentleness when she's around Nan and Pops that she doesn't let show that much around the rest of the group. Pops makes everyone laugh, and Nova has to wipe her eyes when she laughs too hard. I especially like it when she laughs against my shoulder like she's trying to hide her face. I never thought someone with such a tough exterior could be so soft on the inside when she's not worried about keeping a wall up.

Nova and I have made a fort on her bedroom floor out of pillows and blankets with the blankets over our heads held up by her bedpost and her dresser like a tent. We sit in the tent next to each other on pillows and a blanket over our laps. We have some snacks in the fort and her laptop in front of us with a movie on. Nova suggested we watch a movie where the love interests are girls, and I didn't disagree despite my nerves about watching a film like that with her.

It gets to the part where the girls kiss for the first time and I feel myself blushing as I shift in my seat, momentarily looking away from the screen. "Are you okay?" Nova asks, popping a piece of popcorn into her mouth.

I've been watching Nova out of the corner of my eye as she absentmindedly touches the tip of her tongue to her lip ring. She nearly catches me doing it now. I quickly glance back at the screen. "Yeah, I'm just not used to movies like this."

Her eyebrows push together further. "Oh, right, I guess you're used to movies with straight people." She laughs. "Think of this as exposure therapy."

I sigh. "I'd say so. Maybe I could learn something," I joke.

She still looks confused. "Like what, how to kiss? This movie is barely PG13."

The blush hasn't left my cheeks. "Yeah, I mean, I've never kissed anyone, so…" I shrug, attempting to make my comment not seem like a big deal.

She gives me an unbelieving look before she brushes the salt from her hand and pauses the movie. "For real?"

I'm embarrassed now. I'm sure that Nova has kissed girls before. She's probably done a lot more than just kiss. I casually pop a skittle into my mouth, avoiding her eyes. "Whatever. It doesn't matter."

She stops me from pressing 'play' on her laptop. "No, tell me." She's turned towards me now. "You've never been kissed, ever?"

"No," I say shyly. "Are you forgetting about my helicopter parents? Even if I wanted to kiss a boy, I'd have to jump through hoops. With girls, I've never even thought about trying."

She makes a face like she understands what I'm saying and sits back normally in her spot, but she doesn't start the movie back, so the screen is stuck on this weird transition shot of blurred lights. There's this tense feeling between us now and I'm trying not to think about this moment being a moment with her.

After a few beats, she looks at me. "Tell me what you're thinking."

I shake my head, looking away. "I can't."

"Why not?"

I still can't look at her. I can't think about her beautiful eyes on me, or how close her thigh is to mine, or how warm the inside of our tent is despite being completely open on one side. "I don't want to screw anything up."

She takes my hand away from my mouth and keeps my hand in hers. "You can kiss me if you want."

I think I'm imagining the nervousness in her voice like I'm projecting my own feelings onto her, but I hope I'm not. She's looking at me the way she does sometimes like she's asking me a question without saying anything. It catches my breath the way her eyes go over my face. I move closer to her and keep my eyes on her lips, her black lip ring resting in the center of her lip. I wonder if we kissed, could I feel the ring against my own lip?

"Are you sure?" I can hear how shaky my voice is.

"Yes," she whispers.

Her lips are soft against mine and there's this feeling that goes through my body that I've never experienced before. It's this warm tingle that reaches my fingertips and the roots of my hair. I can barely feel the ring on her lip against mine. I've copied her and closed my eyes, letting this feeling wash over me. Her hand is still in mine, and I hold it a little tighter. I wish I could touch her and be closer than we are right now.

She pulls away first. "See?" I open my eyes. "The world didn't end," she smiles.

I swallow nervously. "Wow," I exhale. I'm more nervous than before and I'm hyper-aware of my hand still being clasped in hers.

"Are you okay?" She's smiling and based on her still holding my hand and not seeming disgusted with me, I think she might have enjoyed that too.

I get close to her again, memorizing the curve of her lips. "Can we kiss again?"

When she kisses me, she catches my bottom lip between hers and her other hand is on my cheek. Her tongue flicks against my teeth as she finds my tongue with hers. She brushes my hair back with her fingers.

"Casey." My name is like honey in her mouth.

When we lay in her bed after spending the evening with Pops and Nan in the living room watching TV together, Nova's hand finds mine beneath the covers. I reach up with my pinky and I feel my hairband on her wrist. She hasn't taken it off since she took it from my hair the other day and I've noticed that she plays with it to keep her hands busy or when we're in the car stopped at a red light.

I stare up at the ceiling, trying to think of what to say to her now that we're in the dark and alone with her grandparents asleep on the other side of the house. She turns on her side and I can feel her staring at me.

Her thumb rubs the side of mine. "You know, for a marshmallow, you're kind of stiff right now." I can tell she's joking and her calling me a marshmallow is an attempt to lighten the mood.

I lay on my side, facing her, keeping my hand clasped in hers. "I'm sorry. I'm a little confused, I guess."

"Did I do something to confuse you?"

"You kissed me," I say softly. "And even though it was great and I'd love to do it a lot more, I'm just wondering why you kissed me in the first place."

She inches closer and I feel her knee pressed against mine. "Because I wanted to," she smiles. "Is that not reason enough?"

I sigh. "Yeah, it is." I start to move away. "Just forget I said anything."

She stops me from turning over. "No, talk to me. You're obviously having some second thoughts about it."

"It's not second thoughts." It's me pulling the reigns on myself. I don't want to think that this is something it's not, so if it's just a kiss, I need her to tell me that. "I need you to tell me exactly what this is."

She lifts our hands up to be on the pillow between us, clasped, making a point. "This is me, and you, together."

"But, why me? I've seen the girls at those shows. They're like you. They're tough and beautiful and the kind of girl I thought you'd go for. Why would you ever choose me over them?"

She kisses the back of my hand. "Because I like you." I wait for her to say something else, but she doesn't.

"There has to be more to that."

She smiles. "Why? I like you, like, really like you. It's pretty simple if you think about it."

"I guess it is." I settle into my pillow, feeling less nervous now. There's still a feeling there, a little bit of doubt that I'm enough for her, but I can't let those thoughts ruin this. She's kissed me more than once and that's enough for me right now. "I really like you too."

"I know." She kisses my forehead, then flips back onto

her back, our hands going back beneath the covers.

    I lay my head on her shoulder and put an arm around her. We lay still for a while and I feel her chest rise and fall with her breaths. They slow and I think she's asleep. I'm nearly asleep when I remember that we were watching a movie earlier that we never finished.

    "Nova," I whisper. "How does that movie end?"

    "Like all lesbian movies end," she whispers. "Tragically."

10

    Nova and I are in her room after school doing homework and I'm desperately trying not to get distracted by her as she plays with my fingertips. There's music playing over her stereo and I'm regretting being the one who suggested we do schoolwork instead of what she wanted to do, which was anything but. At school, she holds my hand beneath the lunch table while we're with our friends, but that's the most couple-y thing we've done at school. I don't even know if we're a couple, but sitting alone with her now, it feels like we are. When she glances at me, I want to kiss her again, but I'm a little scared.

    Our eyes lock and she smirks, raising an eyebrow. "If you want to kiss me, just do it."

    I lean over and kiss her, dropping my pencil so I can tuck my fingers underneath her hair and pull her closer to me. I can feel her smiling against my lips and her hand goes to my hip, playing with the bottom seam of my shirt. A buzzing noise interrupts us and I realize that it's one of our phones.

    She pulls away from me a little. "I think that's yours."

    I consider pulling her close again and kissing her while I let my phone continue to ring, but since no one really calls me, I know it can only be one of a few people. I groan, separating from her. I dig in my bag and pull out my phone.

    I see Mom on the screen. "My mom's calling me," I tell Nova.

    She looks down at my phone, her eyes wide with shock. "Are you going to answer?"

    Neither of my parents has called me since they kicked me out of the house. I half expected my mom to call and apologize, but she didn't even text me to see if I was still alive after that first night. I never expected Dad to care much and after the way my mom reacted to me coming out, I guess I shouldn't have expected her to do anything differently.

I watch my phone for a moment, considering the consequences if I don't answer. There's the looming fear that my parents are going to find me at Nova's, dragging her and her grandparents into this mess. They could also show up at my school if they wanted. Then, there's the fear that they're going to order my being picked up by someone at the conversion camp so they don't have to deal with me.

I put the phone to my ear as I watch Nova nervously. "Hi, Mom," I say into the phone.

"Where are you?" She doesn't sound like how I would expect a mother to sound after not seeing her only child.

"I'm with a friend." I can't shake the nerves from my voice, even though Nova is holding my hand, her thumb rubbing the back of mine for comfort.

"That brown girl?" Mom asks. I see Nova make a face and I'm forced to apologize with my own look.

If I tell Mom that I'm with Nova, or who Nova is, she's going to figure out where I am and show up here. "Why are you calling?" I ask. Nova nods, urging me to ask questions. "I thought you didn't want anything to do with me."

I hear Mom sigh on the other end. "You're a minor, Casey. You can't be on the street."

"I'm not on the street," I remind her. "I never had to be." I tighten my grip on Nova's hand. "I had someone care enough to take me in."

"You need to come home," Mom snaps. "We won't look unfit because of a rebellious phase you're going through."

"It's not a phase," I say confidently.

"Casey Hope Walker." My dad's voice comes over the phone. I didn't realize Mom had me on speaker. I can imagine my dad biting his tongue while Mom spoke until he couldn't hold it anymore. "If you aren't home by dinner, we're calling the police and they'll bring you home. Do you understand?"

I know he means it. They might not be able to figure out where I am, but I know the cops would be able to. I can feel the tears brimming my eyes and I release Nova's hand to wipe my eyes. "I understand," I whisper. I hang up the phone before they can say anything else.

Nova reaches forward and wipes a tear from my cheek. "What's going on?"

"They're making me come home." I can't control the tears now and I pull my knees to my chest. "I have to leave."

She wraps her arms around me and puts her lips against my head. "I thought they didn't want you home?"

"I thought so, too, but I think they're more afraid of being seen as failures as parents than they're afraid of having a gay kid." I lean my head into her and sob.

"They can't make you come home," she says defiantly. "I won't let you go somewhere you're not accepted."

I hold her close. "They'll send the cops after me if I'm not home by dinner. I'm a minor, so I have to do what they say."

"Fuck the cops," she groans. "We'll figure this out, okay?"

I sigh against her. "Just hold me, please."

A little while later, after sobbing into Nova's shoulder as she held me and soothed me, we came to the conclusion that we couldn't run away, even if Nova did suggest it more than once. Nan and Pop are sitting in the living room and I know I have to tell them what's going on. After Nova helps me tell them my situation and I thank them profusely for everything they've done for me, I can tell they're both upset for me.

"We're always here for you," Nan says. She'd echoed Nova's feelings about me having to leave, but then she conceded that I had to do what's best for my safety.

Pops smiles at me the way he does like I'm in his blood. "I support this," Pops says, eyeing me and Nova. "I think you make a cute couple." He always knows what to say to make me feel better.

Nan nods. "Absolutely." She eyes me. "It's not fair to you

that you have to pretend, you know that."

I hold onto Nova a little tighter. "But I just got her," I say to Nan, attempting to keep the pitiful tone out of my voice.

Nova grins at me and then kisses my cheek. "You have me."

Nova and I are sat in her car at the corner of my street. She'd wanted to drive me all the way to my house, I think just to show her face to my parents and maybe even give them the finger, but I wouldn't let her. I have to keep her safe just like she wants to keep me safe. As I'd packed my things, Nova sat on her bed spouting how much she hated my parents and trying to grab me and hold me as much as she could before we were forced to leave.

She's quiet now, which is uncharacteristic of her, as she bites on her lip next to her lip ring. I think she's in denial, or maybe she's waiting to see how long it takes for someone to force me out of her car. I can only hold her hand as she silently seethes. Her lip quivers and I can tell she's close to tears, just like I am. Unlike me, she's fighting it, though, I think for my benefit.

She takes a deep breath before she releases the steering wheel. She turns to me and I can see the evidence that tears were seconds away from spilling over her eyes. She leans across the console and brushes my cheek with her fingers as her eyes are locked onto mine. "I love you."

I kiss her, holding her to me, hoping that if I hold her tight enough that she'll absorb into me and I can take her along with me. "I love you, too."

♀

My parents are stood by the stairs when I walk in. I know I'm not late, but they're looking at me like I am. I lower my bag to the floor and stand by the open door wishing I could turn around and run after Nova letting her take me somewhere we can be together where no one will find us. She loves me, and despite anything that's going to happen now, I know I have that.

Dad has his arms crossed over his chest. He nods toward the dining room. "We need to talk."

I don't move. "You asked me home and I'm home. Talking wasn't part of the agreement." I know I can't lay over easily because they won't believe it. I can't say 'well, being away from home has cured me and I'm straight now. Thank god that phase is over. No worries, Mom and Dad.'.

Dad thrusts a finger toward the dining room. "Now, Casey."

I do as he says and the three of us go to the dining room. They sit on one side of the table and I sit on the other, just like the day I was forced to come out to them. It feels like sitting in front of judges, which I guess is true since they hold the fate of my life in their hands.

"What do you want me to say?" I ask.

"We don't want you to say anything," Dad says. "We're setting rules from now on."

"Let me guess," I huff. "The first one is, don't be gay."

Neither of them is enthused about my attitude. "You won't be gay in this house," Dad says matter of factly. "There will be no mention of it and whoever that brown girl is, you're not allowed to be around her."

I don't mention that despite their best efforts, Nova and I love each other and no stupid rules are going to change that. I also don't mention that my being gay doesn't stop being a thing when I cross the threshold of the house. Instead, I say nothing.

"You're also grounded," he says, continuing with the rules. "That means you go to school and you come home. Any friends you've made since we've been here are off-limits, especially if these friends are encouraging this lifestyle."

"I'm in prison, I understand," I say flatly.

"And drop the attitude," Dad barks. "That's not how you talk to your parents, or anyone with authority, for that matter."

I look at Mom, who hasn't said anything since I walked in. "Do you have any rules for me, or are you letting him speak for you?"

Mom goes to say something, but Dad interrupts. "Go to your room, Casey." He points his finger toward the stairs. "Your mother will call you down for dinner."

I take my bags upstairs and begin unpacking them. Since I still have my phone, I let Nova know that I'm okay.

Casey: grounded and I can't be gay in the house, whatever that means

I set my phone down and wait for her reply. I start unpacking my things and I find papers folded up and tucked into one of the pockets. I open the papers and a small note falls from between them. It's from Nova.

> Keep these on your wall of shame for me.
> -Nova

I unfold the pages she'd tucked away with the note and I see that they're drawings she's done in the sketchbook I gave her. One drawing is me sleeping in her bed. The others are smaller sketches of things we've talked about like some jellyfish, a heart with our names, and her stereo playing the songs we like, the lyrics flowing from the speakers. I go to my closet and slide my clothes to the side, so I can see the wall where I have the first drawing Nova did of me, the paper with Nova's number, and the photo Kaida took of us, which I'd sneakily printed in the school library. I tack the drawings up on the wall, along with the note, before sliding my clothes back to their place.

Nova has texted me back.

Nova: I have a solution. Talk exclusively about dicks. See how long it takes before your parents are begging you to be gay again

I know she's joking and I laugh.

Casey: I don't think I could keep a straight face

Nova: I'd hope not. I like your gay face

Casey: your gay face isn't so bad either lol thank you for my drawings, btw

Nova: how many more before it becomes a shrine?

Casey: funny of you to assume it's not already

Nova: freak

I never thought houses could hold their own temperature regardless of what a thermostat says, but I can feel the difference between mine and Nova's house, easily. My house is cold, the kind of cold I can feel down in my bones and no matter how many blankets I wrap around me, it's not enough. Nova's house was warm, like the kind of warmth that crawls across your skin when you sit in front of a fire after being out in an abnormally cold day without a coat. Being in her presence makes me feel like my skin is thawing and being back in my home, with parents who might as well be freezer burnt, feels like there's this layer of ice back on my skin.

11

It's the morning of Pride in the city and I have a plan. I was up late last night texting with Nova on how we're going to navigate everything today. I'd been considering not going given how hostile my parents have been towards me lately. When we're forced to be around each other, which is usually just dinner, Dad goes between being deathly quiet and being obnoxious with his jabs toward me that I know he thinks are subtle, but are anything but. Mom is acting like I don't exist. When I walk through the door after having been at school, where I barely get to even look at Nova in case Patrick opens his mouth, Mom doesn't acknowledge me. It's bad enough that I don't get to talk to Nova or anyone else from the group at school, but I've been forced to take the bus again, too.

My parents left early this morning to meet at the church before they all pile into buses and head to Pride with their signs and bigoted attitudes in tow. I wasn't asked if I wanted to go. It was a toss up if my parents were going to keep me from Pride altogether like they always had before, or if given recent changes, they were going to force me to go and hold up a sign I didn't agree with. Luckily, it was the former, and I was threatened if I left the house, God forbid (literally) if I thought about leaving the house to go to Pride. Dad didn't mention me going to Pride, but it was implied by his tone when he said: "and don't even think about leaving this house, young lady.". Given how things have been lately, I didn't argue. I nodded as I sat at my desk with unfinished homework being my alibi.

My parents have been gone for a little over an hour when I climb out of my window in clothes that are going to be easy to get out of. Dad had set the alarms for the house before they left, so going out the front door wasn't an option. I navigate the pellets Dad sprinkled across the room for those raccoons he'd thought were on the roof, something I never corrected. Most of them are gone from the night Nova showed up and she'd had us both on the roof collecting them to protect the squirrels and birds from eating them. It was the only night we'd risked her showing up after about three days of not being able to be around each other except for the times we'd sneak away in school between classes. Girls bathrooms and moldy alcoves aren't the most romantic spots to kiss in.

    I slide into Nova's car and she greets me with a long kiss before she pulls clothes from the backseat of her car. "Luckily, you and Kaida are the same size." She hands me the clothes. "I have these for you, too." She puts a pair of platform sneakers by my feet. "And the cherry on top." She holds a cropped bright pink wig in her hand with straight across bangs. I must be making a face because she laughs. "No one will recognize you. This is what you wanted, right?"

    I look down at the clothes. "I hope it works."

    We meet the rest of the group at the train station where Nova parks the car. I'd managed to change as she drove us. Pulling on fishnet tights and shorts wasn't easy given how many times I'd accidentally put my toes through the small holes, which made Nova laugh as she'd glance at me after I'd groaned a complaint. As we wait on the others, I fix the top Kaida let me borrow, which would make my dad have a heart attack if he knew I was wearing it, but I try not to think about what my parents think of me. Nova helps me tuck my hair beneath the wig and fix the wig to look as natural as possible.

    I put the shoes on and Nova helps me step out of the car to get my balance. I smooth down the shorts—black with hot pink details, and the shirt. Nova is dressed as she normally is, but she's added a bandana around her neck in the colors of the lesbian flag, probably the only time I'll ever see her in pink.

    I lean back against her car and she eyes me. "I like this

look on you."

I playfully roll my eyes. "I'm going to have the weirdest tan lines."

She reaches out her hand to me and I take it. "Do you feel enough undercover?"

"I don't feel like myself if that's what you mean."

"It's just a costume," she assures me. "You're Casey Walker and you're going to Pride with your girlfriend. Say it so you know it's real."

I exhale. "I'm Casey Walker and I'm going to Pride with my girlfriend." The word 'girlfriend' rolls off my tongue and I smile.

Nova does too. "That's better." She kisses me softly. "Those shoes make you my height. I don't like them," she jokes.

Kaida, J.J, and Lars meet us on the platform as we wait on the train. Kaida, dressed like me since I'm wearing her clothes, winks at me. "I knew those would look good on you. You can't keep them, though."

"No worries," I tell her. "And thank you for letting me borrow them."

She smiles smugly. "I knew Nova would've put you in her clothes and let's be honest, her clothes wouldn't exactly flatter your figure."

Nova flips her off with the hand that's not holding mine. I pull the shorts down a little. "I think I miss my blouses," I tell Kaida.

She rolls her eyes. "It's Pride, Casey. It's the one day of the year that you can be a bit more expressive."

J.J puts their hands on the handlebars of Lars's chair when we see the train in the distance. "Expressive," they huff, mocking Kaida. "At least you get to be expressive."

Kaida squints her eyes at him. "Don't play that card with me. You and Lars choose to keep your relationship on the DL."

I look at Nova, confused. "I didn't know they were together," I tell her.

"Almost two years," Nova says.

"Some of us choose to not flaunt ourselves to the world," J.J says. "Privacy is rebellion in the age of social media."

"Here, here," Lars mumbles.

Once we squeeze onto the train, we're all forced to stand due to the number of people who are already on the train, except for Lars. I can tell most of the people on the train are headed to the festival with their rainbow garb, other respective flags, and pronoun pins. Nova and I are pushed close together each holding onto the bar with one hand as the train moves.

Her other arm goes around my waist and I tense. "Are you okay?" Even by my ear, she's hard to hear over the sound of everyone on the train.

I must have been biting my lip with anxiety because my lip feels sore and there's a trace of the taste of blood in my mouth. I loop my finger through her belt loop and offer her a grin, even though I can feel my heart beating in my ears. I try not to let my mind wander to how we'd be trapped on the train if someone decided to hurt us. I push away the thought of a bomb going off or someone pulling a knife.

I feel eyes on us and I nearly release Nova once I make eye contact with two college-aged girls who are practically sitting in each other's laps across from us. The one girl subtly nods at me and the other smiles at me before kissing the first girl on the cheek. Nova's hand is rubbing my side and I realize that where we are, with all of these like-minded people, I don't have to be afraid. I lean over and give Nova a quick kiss on her cheek. Someone has started to play dance music from a portable speaker and as much as they can people start to move along with the music turning the train car into a dance club.

Nova is holding my hand as we walk through the festival. J.J and Lars are next to Nova. Kaida is walking next to me. J.J occasionally pushes Lars in his chair through tight spaces beeping for people to move out of the way. There are a lot of people at the festival of all ages, races, genders (or lack thereof), and sexualities. Some people are dressed simply while others are covered in glitter and not much else.

When we get to the street with the parade, the five of us find a spot a little up a hill for Lars to see above people's heads. Floats go by for organizations in the city, including Planned Parenthood and GLAAD. People on the floats are dancing, waving, and tossing things, like beads and condoms, from the float. Everyone is smiling, happy to represent their organization and generally happy to be here. I'd thought I'd feel afraid being in this big of a crowd, but more than anything, I feel included like I belong somewhere for the first time in my life.

Nova nudges me, pointing in the direction of one of the floats. "Do you remember the woman I told you about that fought for the inclusion of trans people of color?" I nod. "There she is."

I follow Nova's finger to the float with a beautiful black woman standing, waving at people as she passes, along with other people of color on the float with her. "That's amazing," I tell Nova.

After the parade, the crowd disperses onto the street where the floats have been cleared away and the streets around the main street of Pride. There are booths lining the side streets, mostly businesses, and some inclusive churches. There's a group of older women standing in a group to the side with a banner that says, Inclusive Moms. They seem to be hugging strangers, some of which are crying.

I bring Nova's attention to the women. Nova smiles. "They're moms who come to pride to hug LGBT kids who aren't accepted by their own parents or the community." She motions to one of the women. "She hugged me at my first Pride, not because I wasn't accepted, but because I'd overheard her tell the last person she hugged that her son was bullied and died by suicide at fifteen. She comes to help make sure no other kid feels unloved."

I release Nova's hand and go up to the closest woman who isn't busy hugging someone. "Hi," I wave.

The woman, probably around my mom's age, smiles at me. "Hey, sugar." She opens her arms. "Would you like a hug?"

I nod and wrap my arms around her wide body. "You're accepted," she says in my ear. "And you are so loved."

I hug her a little tighter before letting go. I can feel tears stinging my eyes having a woman who was raised in the same time as my mom be so different from her and so loving and accepting of a stranger she's never met, but hugged like we're lifelong friends.

I smile and blink away tears. "Thank you."

She squeezes the top of my arm. "You go have fun, baby."

I find Nova with the woman she'd pointed out earlier, holding her hand as the woman wipes away tears and Nova smiles sympathetically. Nova hugs the woman and I can tell the woman is the one who needed the hug, not Nova.

Nova spots me and grabs my hand again. "I think the others are grabbing some food. Did you enjoy your hug?"

I nod. "I didn't think a hug could do so much. Maybe one day, I can be one of the mom's that comes to Pride and hugs the kids who need it."

"You should," she agrees.

We get further down the parade and before we can even see them, I can hear the protestors, my parents among them, shouting at the festival-goers walking by. By the look on Nova's face, I know she can hear them too. We can't avoid them because of where they're placed. Nova holds my hand a little tighter as we get closer to the protestors. We keep our distance and I keep my face hidden as much as I can while my eyes search the group for my parents and anyone I recognize from the church we go to.

Nova steps in front of my line of sight. "Don't do that to yourself," she tells me. "You already know they're here."

I know she's right, but I can feel this heat creep up my chest that isn't coming from the heat around us from the late summer sun. "Can the protestors see us?" I ask her.

She glances toward the protestors and I see her lock eyes with one of them. He starts yelling directly at her. "I'd say so," she groans. "Why?"

I raise my eyebrows, inviting her in. She places a hand on

either side of my face and I forget every fear I have in my body as I feel her lips on mine. I feel her hand move to the back of the wig as she kisses me deeper. My arms go around her waist. There's no aggression behind her kiss, only love. She's being intentional, but I know it's not for rebellion. I'm not kissing her for that reason either. I don't care about the protestors screaming obscenities at us or the whistles and cheers of the pride goers around us. There's only me and Nova.

♀

It's a couple of hours after Nova has dropped me home from Pride and I'm back in my normal clothes with my normal hair. My phone hasn't stopped going off since our group got back on the train. A lot of people captured the kiss between me and Nova on their phones, and the pictures, which are all from different perspectives, have been shared to social media. Among LGBT groups, the pictures are going viral and as I scroll through each site, the amount of attention the photos are getting is growing. In the replies are tons of comments, good and bad, but most surprisingly, there are comments of news journalists and zine creators asking permission to use the photos to further broadcast Nova and I. Our display is being seen as a form of protest and I'm focused on the comments of people who are inspired by our display.

Since Nova is herself in the photos, not under any sort of disguise like I was, her identity has become known and everyone sharing the photos and commenting below them wants to know more about her. As for me, however, no one knows who I am. The comments are calling me the 'mystery girl', which I have mixed feelings about. There's a part of me who wants to be known as the girl in the photos, not even for any kind of popularity reason, but because I want people to know that Nova is kissing me. The other part, the one that has me rooted to my chair, is glad that I'm being called the 'mystery girl'. If no one can recognize me, it means that my parents, and the rest of the community, can't either.

The only people who know it's me in the photos are my friends, and of course, Nova. I've been put into the group text with everyone in the group and I feel like I can barely get a breath out before one of them is texting again. Kaida keeps sending us screenshots of the different websites. Lars and J.J are talking about how to use the photo for our own benefit, which I'm unsure of, but I don't dare say anything. Nova seems to be just as overwhelmed as I am because every time Kaida suggests Nova make any social media account and take on her newfound local celebrity status, Nova shuts it down completely. Kaida also suggests that I make myself known, but I quickly shoot that down before anyone else can jump on board.

I hear the front door beep downstairs, indicating that my parents have come home, so I silence my phone after sending the group a quick text and open the book on my desk to pretend like I've been doing schoolwork since they left this morning. I can hear my mom's footsteps coming up the stairs and I frantically look around my room to make sure I didn't accidentally leave anything out that would've indicated that I wasn't here. I glance up at the window and see that the lock is undone. She's made it to the top of the stairs. I launch myself up from my desk chair and lock the window before I crash back into my seat, catching my breath and slowing my heart back down to a reasonable rate.

When she opens my door, I inhale as I turn in my chair. "We're home," she says flatly.

"Okay." I exhale slowly, watching her face for any sign that she knows. When she doesn't yell at me or indicate that she does, I allow myself to relax a little.

"Dinner will be in an hour." There's this look on her face like she's talking to a stranger. I notice she can't look at me, much less in my eyes. She's watching the floor and keeping one hand on the doorknob like she's itching to close the door and forget that I'm here.

"Mom." I catch her before she starts closing the door. I

wait for her to look at me. "Do you hate me?"

    Her eyes flick back down to the floor. "I think you should pray, Casey." She shuts the door and I hear her walk back down the hallway.

13

By lunch at school on Monday, the picture of me and Nova has been seen by everyone and I have a nervousness growing in my stomach when I see Nova. It feels weird that after this weekend I'm still having to sit alone at lunch, only being able to watch my friends and Nova sat at their usual table. J.J has their usual cigarette in their mouth, Lars is on his old school laptop typing away, Kaida is braiding her hair absentmindedly as she's talking to Nova, and Nova is picking at the crust of her cheese pizza as she's laughing at something Kaida said. She's trying to keep me included in the conversation by texting me to keep me in the loop, but it's not the same. I feel like I'm staring in on the life I want, but I can only sit on the outside and watch this life continue without me.

Multiple people come up to Nova when she's standing in the hallway and ask her about the picture. I can only stand and watch as some of them fawn over her, treating her like a celebrity or begging for her to tell them the identity of the other girl in the photos. She doesn't, of course, and I can tell she's feeling a bit weird about her sudden popularity at school. The ones who don't think of her as a hero, including Patrick, don't dare say anything to Nova, but they shoot daggers at her with their eyes and make snide comments to each other, but not loud enough to Nova to hear them.

By the middle of the week, her stardom has faded a little, but there's a growing need to figure out who the other person in the photos is. All over social media, more and more people are asking who the girl with Nova is, even posting some pictures of potential girls who have my jawline or the same curve in my nose. Some of them are reposting the picture with yearbook pictures of random girls that go to our school, and surrounding schools, to try and figure it out. I know they're getting close to figuring it out and I know that if anyone posted a picture they took from any other time at Pride when Nova and I were walking hand in hand or when her arm was around my shoulders, it would be obvious that the girl in the kissing picture with Nova is me.

On Friday morning, Mom is standing at the bottom of the stairs with her arms crossed over her chest as if she was waiting for me to come downstairs on my way to school. Her eyes are intense and she's watching me, unblinking. I hold the strap of my bag as I pause on the middle step waiting for an explanation. Upon further inspection, I see her phone clawed in her hand, her knuckles white from holding the phone so tightly.

"Is everything okay?" I ask quietly.

She brings her phone up and turns the screen toward me. "How long did you think you could hide this from us?"

I have to take a few more steps down to be sure I'm seeing what I'm seeing on her phone screen. It's the picture that's been posted and reposted hundreds of times across social media sites. I can feel the color drain from my face and my mouth suddenly feels dry along with a heaviness in my chest.

"Who is that?" I ask, still trying to keep my composure.

If my mother was a violent woman, I swear she'd reach out with her other hand and smack me across the face. Her eyes are doing it for her, though. "You don't think I wouldn't recognize my own daughter?" She takes the phone back and tucks it under her arm, continuing to grip the phone as if I'd snatch it from her hand. "We trusted you, Casey, but you've continued to lie to us."

I think back to Pride when the woman wrapped her arms around me and assured me that I was loved. I long to be back there now, a stranger and mom to another child telling me the things I wish my own mother would say to me right now. My thumb goes to my mouth and I accidentally bite my thumb harder than I intended, which makes tears come to my eyes. "Does Dad know?"

"No," she says sharply. "If he did, you'd be in the car on your way to camp before you could blink."

I swallow nervously. "Are you going to tell him?"

Her hand loosens slightly on the phone and her eyes go to the ground before they come back to me. "On Monday, you'll be headed to Brunswick Christian School, like we intended in the first place. A spot opened and I took the money to the school myself yesterday afternoon."

My chest feels like a balloon that has just deflated. "You're pulling me out of my school? That's not fair. I'm making good grades and I've settled."

"You broke our trust, Casey." She shrugs like she doesn't care what I have to say. "I'm ironing your uniform pieces this weekend and tomorrow we'll go out and get you some sensible stockings and shoes, both of which have been recommended by the woman at the front desk." She starts to turn away.

"Does Dad know why I'm changing schools?"

She eyes me. "A spot opened up," she says flatly.

I continue to feel the panic rising in my chest and the tears are threatening to spill over my bottom lashes. "Making me go to that school won't make me straight."

Her eyes narrow slightly. "Until you're on your own, you are the good straight Christian girl we've raised you to be. If that doesn't work for you, the camp is only one phone call away. I know you don't want to go there, so I'm giving you a choice. School or camp." She's waiting impatiently for my answer as she taps a finger against the back of her phone.

"School," I stammer.

She nods once. "I thought so." She motions toward the door. "Your bus will be here soon. You don't want to be late on your last day."

I'm waiting by Nova's locker when I see her coming down the hallway, which is starting to fill up with students as the ringing of the first bell approaches quickly. She looks confused to see me. "Casey, I thought we had to be sneaky from now on." There's a smile in her tone as she stands in front of me, hooking her pinky with mine.

I pull her to me and kiss her in front of everyone. I don't care about who sees us anymore or if everyone in the school knows that I'm the girl in the pictures from Pride. I want people to know that I love her and no matter what happens, I'm not ashamed to be the girl in the photos.

She pulls away as we hear cameras on phones snapping and the wave of conversations that are happening. Her eyes don't leave mine. "What's going on?"

I glance around at the phones pointed at us and the eyes that are watching us as each person talks to their neighbor. They finally know who the girl in the pictures is and she's been here right in front of them the whole time. The photos they've taken are going to get posted and spread around just like the Pride photo, which means my mom will probably see it, but I don't care. She can rip me from this school, force me to wear a uniform at another school, and shove her beliefs down my throat all she wants to, but my love for Nova isn't going to change and she needs to know that.

I take Nova's hand and we ignore as the first bell rings, warning us that we only have a few minutes to get to class. As the other students start to move towards their classes, I lead Nova to one of our usual secret places.

We're alone in the small alcove and she's waiting on an explanation. "My mom figured out it was me in the photo," I tell Nova. "Today is my last day at MLK. On Monday, I go to Brunswick Christian."

Her jaw slacks a little and her eyes shift from confusion to anger. "How can she do that? That's not fair."

"I know," I exhale. "It was either Brunswick or camp, so I

chose Brunswick."

Nova drops my hand and begins to pace around the small space we're in. "She can't do that. She can't pull you out of one school and drop you into another one. It'll take you forever to catch up at Brunswick. Does she not realize that?"

"She doesn't care. She wouldn't care how long I've been in this school. A spot was open, she paid them money, and picked up my uniform. That's it."

Nova's eyes widen. "I forgot those douchebags wear uniforms." She groans. "Was she serious when she said you had to choose between the school and camp?"

I nod. "I wouldn't call her bluff about the camp, anyway. She made it sound like my dad was prepared to pack my bags for me before carting me off." My thumb goes to my mouth and Nova immediately brings my hand back down to her belt loop. "I wish things could be different." I look down at her boots. "If you want to end things, I know this isn't what you signed up for."

She tilts my chin up with the side of her other finger, forcing my eyes to hers. "You don't get to push me away because you think I'm going to push away first." She kisses me lightly. "I'm not going away, regardless of the time we see each other now. You're stuck with me."

By lunch, there are side-by-side comparison photos of the photos of me and Nova at Pride being compared to the photos of the kiss we had in the hallway this morning. Everyone in school and anyone else following the Pride photo saga knows that the other girl in the pictures is me. The sudden 'fame' is a little overwhelming with my follower numbers climbing on social media and the string of comments going on in not only those photos but my own personal photos that date back to when I lived in Arizona. There are speculations of which of my old friends is the 'ex', which I try to delete, but I'm not fast enough. My phone is buzzing in my pocket at the lunch table with messages from my old friends wanting to know what's going on.

I've decided that since it's my last day at MLK High, there's no reason for me to sit alone at lunch and I'm back with my friends at their table. Nova has spread the word to the group that it's my last day and why. Nova has been extra clingy in the halls, practically holding me to her when we walk and kissing me every chance she gets. Now, I'm practically in her lap as she holds tight to my waist and my head rests on her shoulder, both wishing we didn't have to separate soon.

The last bell of the day rings and as I'm standing by my locker pulling everything from it, including a flannel of Nova's that I had borrowed a couple of weeks back, Kaida practically tackles me with a hug. The rest of the group is right behind her, but she seems to have run the last few feet to reach me first.

She's pinned my arms to my sides as she's hugged me from the side. "I'm going to miss you so much," she squeals. I didn't think Kaida and I were close enough for this kind of touching since we didn't really talk unless Nova was around or we were in the group text, but now she's acting like she's losing her best friend.

I place my bag on the ground and turn enough to hug her back. "I'm going to miss you too, Kaida. There are always shows and things like that," I point out. "If I can get away, that is."

She pulls back and I see that she's frowning. "You've done it before." Her voice is full of hope.

"That's true," I nod.

J.J raises their fist to me. "It sucks you have to leave this place. Lunch won't be the same without giving you shit."

I bump their fist with mine. "I'm sure you'll manage," I joke.

Lars tilts his chin up to me from where he's next to Nova. "See you around." From the little I know about Lars, he doesn't do sappy things, which I guess is why he and J.J are such a good match.

Nova reaches her hand out to me and I take her hand in mine after picking up my bag and closing my now empty locker. She'd convinced me earlier while we were tucked away in an alcove to let her drive me home. At first, I thought it would be a bad idea because I wasn't sure if my mom would be waiting up for me, but then I agreed because I don't really care if Mom sees us or sees the picture from this morning that's been circulating social media. I don't know when I'm going to see Nova after today and I want as much time with her as I can get.

Nova has been grasping my hand in hers and I've been leaning on her bent arm on the middle console as she's driven to my house slower than she needs to, but I think she's making our time together last as long as she can. I wish, as she and I are sat at the usual spot by my house, that I could pause the world around us and the rest of the world would disappear leaving only us inside her car.

I sit up a little, but I keep my hand in hers. "Do you have to go?" Nova asks.

"I have a few minutes."

We don't speak the rest of the time we have left. Instead, we kiss and have our hands in each other's hair and on each other's shoulders, waists, and hips.

14

    My alarm trills me awake early on Monday morning. Over the weekend, Mom dragged me along to three different stores to find the stockings and shoes for my uniform, a more 'sensible' book bag, and anything else she thought would give people the idea that I wasn't coming from what she and Dad described more than once as the 'ghetto school'. She also took me to get my hair trimmed and there was a moment while she wasn't hovering over the hairstylist that I thought about grabbing the clippers in the holder by my knees and shaving the side of my head just to prove body autonomy. I didn't, of course, but as I think about my day ahead, I kind of wish I had.

    Mom had ironed one of my uniforms, the skirt and the shirt, last night and it hangs on the back of my door like a grim reminder. After I shower and dry my hair, which is an inch and half shorter than before, I dress in the uniform, stockings and all. I look at myself in my bedroom mirror as I smooth down the blue and green plaid skirt that brushes my knees at the hem. The shirt is a stark white polo with the school's crest on the top of my left breast, also green and blue with an eagle head in the center. I look down at the shoes, glossy black Mary Jane's that remind me of the shoes I had as a child. That's what I feel like in this uniform, like a child being dressed by her mother because she can't be trusted to dress herself.

    It's a requirement that because my hair is long, I have to wear it in a ponytail at the back of my head slicked down on top, which I guess signifies some kind of proper attire. Nova has my favorite hair tie, which she's worn on her wrist since the first night I stayed at her place before we were ever together. I have more boring ones, so that's what I opt for, something plain as to not bring attention to myself. I'd spoken to Nova on the phone yesterday after I got back from church where Mom bragged to everyone that I got into Brunswick Christian, even if we did pay for my admission. Nova told me to keep my head down and blend in, which is the exact opposite of what I thought she was going to say when I mentioned how nervous I was for my first day. She said blending in will make me forgettable, which is what I want to be in the eyes of that school—a ghost.

Mom is waiting for me downstairs. Brunswick Christian School doesn't have public transportation for their students and since I still don't have a car, Mom doesn't have a choice but to drop me off and pick me up every day. There's a small part of me that revels in her being inconvenienced by her own doing. Before I go downstairs, I decide to take a picture of me in the mirror with my uniform. I flip off the mirror with a scowl on my face, snap a picture, and send it to the group.

Casey: crucify me

♀

Brunswick Christian School is a massive brick building with what reminds me of church steeples at the top and exaggerated arches at the main entrance. The building itself, according to the map I'd looked over last night to squelch that aspect of my anxiety, has multiple stairwells, a library that could rival one in a university, and a courtyard with statues and a fountain, which is also where students are expected to eat lunch on nice days, though there is an impressive cafeteria to sit in on cold or rainy days.

On the ride over, Mom had been going on about the 'do's' and 'don't's' of this school, most of which I tuned out because I already know what she's going to say. Still, she's decided that I needed to be reminded a million times by the time we get to the front of the drop off line with the rest of the uniform-clad students. The rules, as I understand them, are as follows:

1. DON'T BE GAY (duh)
2. SAY YOUR PRAYERS (obviously)
3. DON'T EMBARRASS THE FAMILY (wouldn't dream of it)

Mom had already picked up my schedule last week along with everything else I'd need for my classes, so I follow the wave of other students whom I can barely tell one from the other because of the uniforms, the uniformity of hairstyles, and lack of any discernible features like makeup or facial piercings. No one is looking at me or seems to notice me at all, which is exactly what I was hoping for as I find my locker that's in pristine condition and could be newly painted if they all didn't look exactly like mine save for the number plate on the front. I put my things away and go to get the books I'll need for my first class when I remember that instead of class first thing in the morning, Brunswick Christian has a short church service.

I close my locker and follow a small group of people to the sanctuary that has been built inside the main school building on the western side of the school. The blue metal doors remind me of gymnasium doors, but then the inside looks like every church I've been in since I was a kid with the pews on either side of the aisle, an organ at the back, high vaulted ceilings, paper thin carpet below my feet, and a pulpit front and center.

There are some students already inside and I look around to see who looks the friendliest to sit beside since sitting alone isn't an option. One girl with light brown skin and tiny curls springing from the top of her head where her hair can't be forced down in its ponytail catches my eye as I walk the aisle. It's not exactly friendly, but I don't have much choice since the pews are filling and the crowd in the aisle is thinning. I slide into the pew with her keeping a respectable distance, but not too much in case she finds my distance to be offensive.

I offer a shy smile and she does it back before her eyes go to the front of the sanctuary, obviously not wanting to talk.

The Wall of Nova

A group comes into the sanctuary and based on how they're louder than anyone as they laugh and seem to have no regard for others, plus the way they walk with a swagger, I know those are the popular kids at this school, which is something I never paid attention to at MLK High. A teacher behind them, an older woman with what appears to be a permanent scowl on her face dressed in a long skirt and blouse buttoned to her neck, hushes them loudly and they make faces at each other like they can't believe someone thinks they can shush them.

The group sits in the pew behind me and this girl next to me. There are three guys, one of which seems to be the leader of the pompous group, and two girls, one who has this glint in her eyes like she'd kill anyone who crossed her, the other more sheepish. The three guys are whispering to each other about a party they went to over the weekend and one of them mentions making out with a really drunk girl, which turns my stomach a little. I make a mental note to avoid them at all costs.

As the rest of the sanctuary fills, the bell rings above us, but it's not the sharp tinny bell I'm used to. It's a rhythmic song that seems to be playing on low soft bells and if it wasn't signifying the start of a school day, I'd think it was peaceful. When the bell ends after about fifteen seconds, the sanctuary is full and there's a hush over the students as the man whom I presume to be the principal/pastor, Dr. Riddick, walks from a door behind the pulpit and up to the podium, scanning his eyes over the students. He has thinning dark hair combed back and a clean-shaven face, a few wrinkles showing on his middle-aged face.

"Good morning," Dr. Riddick says, his voice booming through the mounted speakers from the microphone clipped to his lapel.

"Good morning," the group echoes.

Dr. Riddick's eyes scan the group and his eyes land on me, which makes a chill run down my spine. "I see a new face in the group today."

A similar callout happened on the first day of being at our new church when we moved here and just like before, it seems like everyone moves in one direction or the other to get a look at the newest face—mine. A few whispers erupt from the pews and it's only a few seconds before I hear the word "picture" be whispered from one person to the other. I should've known the picture of me and Nova would follow me here.

Dr. Riddick clears his throat, which makes the whispers stop. His eyes are still on me. "Everyone give a warm welcome to our newest student and follower of Christ, Casey Walker."

There are a few restrained claps and a few murmured "hello"'s. Someone pretends to cough as they say "gay" loud enough for everyone to hear, which makes others laugh. So much for Mom's plan. Everyone here already knows about me. I doubt I'll be able to go anywhere in this town without everyone having seen the pictures of me and Nova.

Dr. Riddick clears his throat again and I think he's going to shame me in front of everyone or ask me to go back to his office where he'll inevitably kick me out of school and force my parents to send me to camp, but then his eyes drop to the podium and he flicks open the Bible in front of him. "Psalms 23, verses one through six." His words are a cue for everyone to grab their bibles from the wooden holders on the backs of the pews in front of them and I do the same as an excuse to keep my head down.

I feel a tap on my shoulder as I have the Bible opened in my hands and my eyes are following the words Dr. Riddick is reciting, even though I know them by heart. I glance over my shoulder to see the head of the group behind me, a boy with straw blonde hair coifed to the side and a wide nose, leaned up to talk to me.

He gestures to the pew in front of me. "Hand me one." I notice he doesn't say "please" and I doubt he's ever used the word in his life. I grab him one of the Bibles and hand it back. I think he's going to sit back and end the conversation, but he doesn't. "That picture was a prank, right?" He's whispering in my ear as I look back down at the words in front of me.

I glance back at him, fully intending to confess my love

for Nova and that the picture wasn't a prank in the slightest, but then his bright blue eyes catch mine and I know that if I say the wrong thing my life at Brunswick Christian will be my own personal hell, even more so than I already know it will be. He's not asking because he's curious. He's baiting me, waiting for a reason to tease me. He could be giving me an out, to settle the rumors about me and make my life a little easier, but I doubt it.

I panic and before I can think it through my brain forces me to say, "Yeah, it was a prank."

He exhales a laugh. "I knew it."

He finally leans back away from me and I go back to looking down at the Bible in my hands, hoping I didn't do something wrong. Nova had told me to keep my head down and to keep myself safe at this school and that's what I'm doing, but there's a pang of guilt that sits in my chest having denied how much Nova means to me.

15

Back in Arizona, I'd gone to public schools because the best Christian schools were Catholic and my parents didn't want me in Catholic school since it was so different from the churches they'd grown up in. Even at the public schools, however, there were a lot of kids from the church my parents raised me in and a lot of underlying religious tones in the curriculum, even though it was frowned upon by the government and the parents of some of the kids in school.

Growing up in those public schools, I didn't have to wear a uniform or attend a morning prayer as I do at Brunswick. I also had my group of kids from my church, so even though we weren't bombarded by Christian ideals in the hallways and in our classes, we were Christian kids who had a reputation for being 'bible thumpers'. I always felt safe in my school having my friends around me and I felt I had a place in the school being in a Christian club and being beloved by a few of my teachers who were the ones to slip in their own beliefs into the curriculum.

Brunswick Christian, on the other hand, has a common vein going through every subject and classroom. In my classes, religion is talked about openly and encouraged as long as the right questions are asked. In the hallway are Christian motivational posters that remind me of the graphics my mom makes to be put on canvas bags, Bible covers, and those yard flags people put in the middle of their gardens. Every aspect of the school feels like a glimpse of the country if our government ran like a theocracy. Having it around every corner and every book I open is a bit smothering, but I don't say anything, of course, not that I have anyone to complain to since the only kid who's talked to me was the boy looking for a reason to pick on me about mine and Nova's picture.

Lunch rolls around and I go to the girl's bathroom to check my phone. I have a string of texts in the group from this morning are more comments about my picture.

>Kaida: cute!

>J.J: stick it to the man!

>Lars: give them hell lol get it?

>Nova: I gotta admit, I don't hate the uniform ;)

I begin to smile at the comments from my friends and start to believe that everything is going to be okay, but then I scroll down and read the texts from a couple of hours ago.

>Kaida: A PRANK? What the hell, Casey?

>J.J: not cool, Case

Those are the only texts and I'm starting to freak out. They know what I said to that kid this morning. I didn't think that my comment would get back to them and I'm still not sure how it did. I don't think anyone at this school talks to anyone at MLK High. I remember where the pictures have been shared and I scroll through the comments beneath the second picture. Sure enough, there's a comment from the kid who talked to me earlier whose name is apparently Liam. The comment where he's telling everyone what I told him in morning service has hundreds of 'likes'. There are comments below his calling me and Nova names, but most of the hate seems to be directed at me.

I have to get to lunch, but I need to make sure Nova doesn't hate me. I can't call her because phones aren't technically allowed in school, even at lunch, so I text her. I don't reply to the group, but to Nova directly.

>Casey: I'm sorry I told Liam our kiss was a prank. I didn't realize

people here would know about the picture. I had to protect myself. I hope you understand

    I don't have time to wait for her to reply and I turn my phone off before I throw it in my locker before I head to lunch. I don't feel very hungry as I go through the line and grab some salad and a slice of pizza, which is name brand by the looks of the boxes stacked in the kitchen on the other side of the line. I think back to my phone in my locker and I wonder if Nova is going to respond and if she does if the response is going to be a good one.

  I walk outside to eat hoping to find a table to sit at alone while I wait for the clock to run out so I can get back to my locker and quickly check my phone before my next class. The tables are occupied and I know I'll have to opt to sit at the end of a table, hopefully unnoticed. I can feel people watching me and even though the rumors about the pictures have been mostly laid to rest, I know that the pictures are going to remain a topic of interest and probably be the biggest part of my reputation as long as I'm at Brunswick.

    I spot the girl I sat next to at morning service eating lunch with a couple of people and my eye catches hers. "Hey, Casey," A voice calls from across the courtyard.

    I recognize Liam's voice from this morning. I think about ignoring him, but now everyone is watching me and I don't want to become an enemy of Liam's, or the rest of his group. I turn my attention toward him and he's waving me over to their table. I make a beeline over there and linger by the table as I wait for him to say something else.

    "Sit," Liam orders.

    I sit next to one of the other guys, a guy with rich brown hair cut short and teeth that are spaced apart. One of the girls, the one with reddish blonde hair, is sat across from me. Liam is in the middle on the other side of me with the other guy on his other side. The other girl, who has cropped brown hair and circle-rimmed glasses is sitting across from him.

The girl across from me eyes me like she's trying to figure me out. "So, that kiss was a prank, huh?" She smirks. "Wanna kiss me next?" She licks her red lips and winks. She obviously doesn't care about the 'no makeup' rule at school. A warmth crosses my face and my lower back.

"Settle down, Kallie," Liam tells her, glaring at her. His eyes go to me. "She's joking. She'll do anything to piss off her parents."

I laugh nervously. "It's fine." I look around at the other tables to see if anyone has noticed me with the popular kids, but no one seems to care.

"Got somewhere to be?" Liam asks.

"No," I say quickly. "I'm just taking it all in, I guess."

This courtyard is so much different than the one at MLK. The concrete is in pristine condition and it looks like it's been power washed recently. The fountain has angels and reminds me of ones that would be in Rome, not that anyone here seems enamored by it. Even the tables seem brand new and unlike the ones at MLK, I don't have to be concerned about needing a tetanus booster.

Liam nods, approving of this answer. "I'm Liam, by the way. You know Kallie."

Kallie smiles flirtatiously at me. "She's going to." Liam side-eyes her.

"Henry," the other guy on Liam's side says. He has fire red hair and enough freckles that his face is nearly brown from them.

"Jill," the girl with circle-rimmed glasses says.

The guy next to me puts his hand out toward me. "I'm Nate." I recognize his voice as the one who made out with the drunk girl at that party last weekend and I subtly scoot myself an inch away from him before carefully shaking his hand.

"Casey," I tell all of them. "But you already knew that."

Liam glances around at the group as if he's reading each of their faces, a silent vote. Finally, he smirks before his eyes go back to me. "Welcome to Brunswick, Casey. I have a feeling we're all going to be great friends."

I smile nervously. So much for keeping my head down.

♀

As it turns out, keeping my head down at Brunswick is proving impossible. After explaining to Nova what happened at Brunswick on my first day and accidentally calling the kiss between us a prank, it seems like she's pumped the brakes a little on our relationship. I don't want to pump the brakes. In fact, I want to press the gas pedal to the floor, but she's made her mind up and there's nothing I can do about that, as much as it hurts. We're still together, I think, but not being able to see each other and our conversations being exclusively through the phone, it's hard for both of us.

Liam, Kallie, and the rest of the group have, for whatever reason, decided to include me in their group, which means we linger in the hallways before morning service, then proceed to saunter in just as the chimes erupt over the speakers, bringing everyone's eyes to us when the heavy doors creak open. It also means sitting with them at lunch and not even getting a moment to myself by my locker or in the bathroom. Kallie seems to be the one to be attached to me most: fixing my skirt when it's folded, lingering by my locker after each class, and looping her arm with mine as we walk the halls or she leads me out of the school to wait on my mom.

On my first day, I wasn't sure what to tell my mom when she picked me up at the front of the school where I was stood with the rest of the car riders. I didn't know if it was safe to tell her that I'd made friends, or at least the closest thing I could get to friends other than my real friends at MLK High. It wasn't until after the third day at Brunswick when Kallie and Liam kept pulling me into the group setting that I was feeling more solid in that I'd found a group to hang out in at Brunswick, even if the relationships had to remain empty and I had to keep pretending to be the person I'm not. Mom had been happy that I'd found friends, of course. The new development had solidified her opinion about Brunswick and she'd gloated a little at dinner that night to Dad who'd taken the idea of Brunswick as his own and nodded, approvingly.

It's Friday at Brunswick and as we sit at lunch, it seems like every table is talking about their weekend plans. Even at my table, Liam and the other guys are talking about some kind of game that's coming on this weekend and it seems important.

Kallie, obviously annoyed at the guys taking over the conversation at the table, clears her throat to get Liam to stop talking, which works. "It's Casey's first Friday night at Brunswick," she says to the group. "What should we do?"

"What we do every Friday night," Henry says like it's obvious. "Luigi's."

Nate nods, agreeing with Henry. "It's a tradition, Kal. We can't break tradition for the new girl." He's talking as if I'm not sitting next to him, but I don't dare say anything that could get me in trouble with the group.

Kallie lowers her eyes on Nate. "I just think we should show her a good time."

"We will," Liam says. He's trying to keep the peace between them. He looks at me. "How does pizza sound to you, Casey?"

All eyes in the group go to me. Jill is grinning at me, I think to alleviate some pressure, but it's not really working. "I'll have to ask my parents," I say softly.

"I'll pick you up," Kallie says like she's not giving me an option. I don't think she is because then the conversation goes back to the previous one and everyone has moved on thinking I'm going to Luigi's with them tonight.

16

    Luigi's is a small pizza place a few miles from Brunswick nestled at the end of a strip mall that includes an office store, a clothing store for middle-aged women, and a nail salon on the other end. The place looks pretty much abandoned except for the parking lot right in front of Luigi's, which is nearly full. Just like she said she would, Kallie picked me up from my house. Before I could go out, my parents wanted to meet her. I'd been nervous not because I didn't think they'd approve, but because Kallie has a tendency to stand close to me and doesn't know how to keep her hands to herself with seemingly anyone she's friends with. Luckily, she'd thrown on the charm around my parents and they seemed to approve of her. I wasn't sure what to wear tonight since none of the kids at Brunswick have seen me out of my uniform and I wanted to fit in. I decided on light colored jeans, a light yellow t-shirt, and sneakers—safe.

    Inside Luigi's, there's a heavy smell of grease and cheese. It looks like almost everyone here tonight is from Brunswick, but they're in normal street clothes. Kallie had slipped off her jeans in her car and changed in the parking lot to a short skirt, something my parents wouldn't approve of and I think Kallie knew that. She also slipped off a light sweater to reveal the tank top beneath, her real outfit tonight. She's showing a good amount of skin and even though I'm not attracted to her in that way, it's hard for me not to stare at her thighs or the few freckles she has on her shoulders around her straps.

    She takes my wrist once we're inside. "I'm sure they've already ordered, so I'll grab some sodas for us."

    I see the rest of the group sat at one of the tables laughing over their own sodas. There are two empty seats, one next to Liam, and the other next to Jill. Liam gestures to the seat next to him, so that's the one I take. I wave to Jill who's anxiously twisting the straw in her can between her thumb and forefinger. She waves with the other hand and bites the tip of the straw between her teeth before taking a sip.

"Welcome," Liam grins. He eyes my hair. "I like it down."

I nervously tuck my hair behind my ear. "Thanks," I mumble.

When the pizza comes to the table, it's massive and there's a pool of grease in the center, which is distributed to the slices when each slice is pulled away onto colorful plastic plates. Kallie has come back with our sodas and as a group we devour the pizza. I don't talk much like I usually don't when we're together, but I find myself laughing at one of Henry's jokes or acknowledging Jill when she's said something the rest of the group doesn't hear. The inside of Luigi's looks like the courtyard at Brunswick with the tables being full of students, but in the closed space there's a low roar of conversations happening between tables, including ours. Before long, people are breaking off from their tables and integrating themselves at other tables. I stay where I am, watching instead.

Our pizza is finished and I'm waiting for Kallie to come back so I can have her take me home for my phone date with Nova, which will be the first time we've talked in the past couple of days. We barely text during the day since I can't have my phone on in class and she hasn't snuck back over since things with my parents are still a bit rocky.

I see a familiar face come into Luigi's. Kaida is squeezing through the Brunswick students on her way to the counter, an annoyed scowl on her face. Some of the Brunswick students are giving her looks like they don't approve of her outfit choice, but she's ignoring them. She gets to the counter and after saying something to the boy working, he goes back to the ovens. Her eyes passively look around the room, then freeze on me.

She looks confused and just as I go to wave to her, her

eyes move from me and back to the guy who's handing her the pizza. She lays down some cash and starts to turn toward the door. Her eyes scan over me one more time and then land on Kallie as Kallie stands next to my seat, her outer thigh on my arm as she leans over and takes a garlic knot from the table. I know I look guilty not because I'm doing anything wrong, but because to Kaida it probably looks like Kallie is more than a friend. I try to stand, intending to go after her, but Kaida is already out of the door.

I stand anyway putting some distance between me and Kallie. "Where are you headed?" Kallie asks, lipping the grease from her thumb.

My eyes glance from her to the door and back. "Bathroom," I lie.

She exhales relieved. "Oh, good. I need to go too." Her arm laces through mine the way she does in the hallway at Brunswick. The crowd seems to part for her when she walks through them. As we pass the windows, I see Kaida standing outside on the sidewalk, her pizza in one hand and her phone in the other. Kallie continues to pull me to the back of Luigi's where the bathrooms are located.

She opens the door and I see that it's a single toilet. I pull my arm from hers. "I'll wait," I offer.

She gestures for me to follow her. "I don't mind."

If I deny her offer now, it'll be awkward, so I follow her inside. I avert my eyes while she goes. "So, hey, there's a party tonight," she says. "It's some kid at Brunswick's brother who has his own place. Are you in?"

She finishes and we switch places, even though I don't have to go. I force myself, anyway. I have my phone date with Nova tonight and after Kaida seeing me with Kallie I'm sure I'll have some explaining to do since I'm pretty sure Kaida was texting Nova earlier.

I fasten my pants and join Kallie by the small sink to wash my hands. "I'm not sure how late I can be tonight. I'm sure you could tell how uptight my parents are."

Kallie catches my eye in the mirror as she dries her hands. "Does this have something to do with that neon nightmare from earlier?"

I didn't realize she saw Kaida or noticed that Kaida saw me. I want to tell Kallie about my date with Nova, but I can't give away my relationship with her. "She's a friend from my old school."

Kallie doesn't seem sure. "She looked pissed."

I shrug, drying my hands. "She usually is," I lie.

Kallie reapplies her red lipstick in the mirror. "She's probably jealous. I mean, she dresses like a cartoon character. It wouldn't surprise me if she was mad because you're with us."

"She's my friend," I defend.

Kallie pauses, rubbing her lips together in the mirror. "Would a real friend be jealous that you found other friends?"

I don't think Kaida is jealous that I'm here with my friends at Brunswick. I think she thinks I'm more than friends with Kallie and that I'm cheating on Nova, but since Kallie and the rest of the group don't know anything about Nova, or that I'm a lesbian, I can't defend Kaida.

Again, I shrug. "I guess not."

Kallie grins, putting her lipstick back in her pocket. She faces me. "I feel like there's so much I don't know about you, Casey Walker." Her hands go to the tops of my arms. "We could be best friends if you want."

I don't know what to say to her. On one hand, it would be nice to have someone to talk to at Brunswick, even if I can't talk to her about certain things. On the other hand, I'm hoping that Brunswick is temporary, so I shouldn't be making anyone who's an acquaintance into a friend. Still, the way she's looking at me, maybe I could get to the point of trusting her, especially if I'm stuck at Brunswick.

"Okay," I say softly.

She smiles. "Secret for a secret?" I nod, nervously. She lowers her lips to my ear. "I'm a virgin."

She pulls back, waiting on my reaction. "Me too," I grin.

"Thank God," she sighs, releasing my arms. "I thought I was the last one in our class." She loops our arms again. "Come on, bestie. If we're in her much longer, someone's going to start a rumor about us." She laughs at the idea.

♀

Everyone in the group seems to be on board with going to this party at some older guy's house and since Kallie and I are supposedly 'bestie's' now, I know I can't back out of this party. It's been determined that we're all going to follow Liam to the party in our respective cars since he's been to this house before. Jill had driven her own car and had brought Henry along with her since she and he are neighbors. Nate rides with Liam.

As Kallie and I are sat in her car waiting on Liam to lead the line, I send Nova a text apologizing for missing our date. "Texting that girl from earlier?" Kallie asks, having flipped down the visor to fix her mascara.

I quickly get back an 'ok' from Nova and nothing else, which makes my heart sink a little. I put my phone away. "No, someone else." Kallie, thankfully, doesn't pry.

The party is outside the small house and no one seems to be going inside, but staying in the front yard between the cars and a bonfire instead. Some of the older people who seem to know the host are sat around the bonfire in lawn chairs holding cups or cans of beer. There are other Brunswick kids here, too, but I only know my group, so I stick close to Kallie. Most of the people at this party seem to be older, the original people invited to the party. I can't figure out who the host is, but it's obvious that some of the older crowd don't like that there are teenagers crashing the party.

Kallie and I each grab a drink. Kallie has taken it upon herself to mix my drink for me, and one sip tells me that it's mostly liquor and not much soda. I know I'm going to have to nurse the drink and think of a way to pour out most of it so that Kallie doesn't notice. Jill has joined us in the yard where we're leaned back against Kallie's car watching the rest of the party as the older people mostly steer clear of the teenagers who have taken over the seats around the bonfire.

Liam approaches us. "Hi, ladies." His eyes go to me. "I need to borrow Casey for a few minutes," he tells Kallie and Jill. Kallie gives him an annoyed look. "I promise I'll bring her back," he tells her.

I offer Kallie a grin. "Be right back," I reiterate.

"Let's take a walk," Liam says, placing his hand on my back.

He leads me away from the main party and into the small house, which is mostly empty. There are a few people smoking on the couch in the living room, but they don't seem to notice us walking through the house. I can feel my nerves firing up and I wish Kallie would've come with us.

We go into a bedroom down the hall and Liam locks the door behind me. I nervously stand by the door as he goes further into the room. "What's up?" I attempt to ask casually.

He sits on the edge of the bed and pats the spot next to him for me to sit. I don't want things to be awkward between us, so I do keeping about a foot of space between us. He takes my drink, which I've managed to empty halfway in the grass outside and sits it on the side table.

He props his leg up to close the space between us. "Having fun?"

I keep my eyes on his hands. "I guess so."

He touches my knee. "Want to have more fun?" Before I can say no, he's kissing me.

I push his chest, pushing him back. There's this feeling that goes through me like I want to hit him, or maybe scream, but I do neither because I'm too shocked to move. "Why did you do that?"

He seems surprised. "I thought you liked me."

"I don't," I say angrily. I scoot back until I'm nearly off the end of the bed. "Not like that."

He eyes me, still confused. "Why not? I thought we were

cool."

I continue to keep my eyes on his hands, waiting on him to lunge at me, to try and touch me or kiss me again. "Because..." I sigh, not wanting to say anything else.

"You're gay." He doesn't phrase it as a question. He's confident that it's the truth. "Those pictures from before, the ones of you kissing that goth girl, that wasn't a prank, was it?"

He's found me out. I thought I'd have more time at Brunswick to convince my parents that I was okay to go back to public school with my other friends and with Nova. A week has to be a record for leaving one school and then re-enrolling.

I plead with him with my eyes. "You can't tell anyone, please. If my parents think I'm still gay, my life will be over." He doesn't realize how true that is.

He considers my plea. "I won't tell anyone," he finally says. "But there's something I need from you." I nod, carefully considering what he's going to ask. I'm willing to do just about anything, but there's a line I won't cross. "My parents need to think I've found a good girl to settle with. Since you have to pretend to be straight, let's make a deal."

I already know that making a deal with Liam is a mistake, but I've run out of options. I guess I should consider myself lucky that all he wants to do is pretend and not force me into something bad. My parents haven't loosened the reigns on me that much, and I know they'll only loosen them further if they think I have a boyfriend. If they think that I haven't gone back to my factory settings of being straight, they'll pack my things and I'll be on the first ride out to that awful place by tomorrow morning.

I exhale trying not to think about the consequences of what I'm about to agree to, or who it's with. "Fine, we can pretend," I emphasize that last part. "But, I won't kiss you, or anything like that. I draw the line at hand-holding and the occasional hug."

He extends his hand out to me the way I've seen my dad do when he's making a deal with investors. From what I know about Liam, his dad is in a similar line of work, so he's probably learned the same mannerisms from him, "Deal." I shake his hand. "Honestly, I'm kind of glad you're gay because if you weren't, it'd be a hit to my ego if you didn't want me."

I can't tell if he's being cocky for the sake of a joke, or not, but I laugh anyway. "Yeah, lucky you, then."

He laughs a little too, but I think he was being serious. "What are the chances that I could get away with hooking up with a college girl at this party?"

I stand from the bed. "Slim given that we're not exactly welcome here. But, if by some miracle you do, maybe don't creepily lock her in a bedroom and kiss her without her permission. That's a lawsuit waiting to happen. Also, it's a terrible thing to do."

He stands from the bed and makes a show of unlocking the door. "You're right." I'm not sure which part he's talking about, but I hope it's the latter. "Let's go, girlfriend. We have some people to convince."

For the rest of the party, Liam and I stay hand in hand unless he's pulled away by Nate or Henry. Kallie seems surprised that Liam and I are 'together', but she doesn't say anything until she's driving me home. She's not drunk and I'm starting to think that she didn't drink at all tonight.

"I didn't know you liked Liam." Based on her tone, I can tell she doesn't believe that Liam and I are together.

I try to think of something a straight girl would say about Liam, like one of the many underclassmen girls I've seen fawning over him in the hallway. "He's the most popular boy at Brunswick. He's charming and he makes me laugh."

Her eyebrows raise, then she nods. "Yeah, I can see that, I guess." There's something else in her tone and I see this look on her face that disappears as fast as it had appeared like she's disappointed.

Kallie drops me off at the bottom of my driveway to avoid pointing her headlights into the house. She doesn't say much as I start to leave the car. Just a casual "see you Monday" before she faces forward again, obviously annoyed.

The house is dark and quiet since my parents are asleep and probably have been for a while. I head upstairs to my bedroom ready to crawl into my bed and pass out after tonight's craziness. I close my bedroom door quietly and flip on the light. I jump when I see Nova sitting on my bed.

"Nova," I breathe. "What are you doing here?"

I can't read her expression. "Kaida told me she saw you at Luigi's with your Brunswick friends. You could've told me you were with them tonight. I wouldn't have been mad."

I feel a little more at ease knowing she doesn't hate me, yet. "Did she mention anything about Kallie?" I don't know if it's smart to seemingly incriminate myself, but I figure if I ask upfront she'll know I have nothing to hide.

"That's her name?" Nova asks flatly. "Kaida says she's pretty."

"She's just my friend," I defend. "She doesn't do boundaries that well, but I promise there's nothing going on between us."

Nova eyes me for what seems like a long time but is really only a few seconds. "Yeah, I know. You're not the type." She seems to relax a little. "Still, you could've told me about her."

"I wasn't sure what to say," I admit. "Kaida's right, she is pretty. She's also smart and has more personality than should be allowed to be in a single person." I smile. "She wants us to be besties, which is nice since I thought I wouldn't have any friends at Brunswick."

Nova smiles too. "I'm glad you have a friend there, genuinely. When I suggested you keep your head down, I only meant to keep yourself safe. I never wanted you to feel alone or like you weren't allowed to be close to anyone but me."

I didn't realize until now that part of the reason I wasn't allowing myself to have friends at Brunswick was that I was afraid to lose Nova. It seems stupid now to think she'd be upset with me having friends, but I guess I thought that she'd want to forget about me if I'm spending my free time with other people.

I cross to my bed in my sock feet, frowning in apology. "I'm sorry I've been distant lately."

She takes my hand in hers. "A lot has changed in your life in a very short amount of time. I'm still shocked that you went to Pride." She smiles. "You don't need to apologize for anything."

My heart swells at how much I love her. "I've missed you, so much."

"I've missed you more."

I lean down and kiss her. Then, I remember the party. "I need to tell you something at the risk of you never wanting to see me again."

Her eyebrows raise. "You didn't kiss her, did you?"

"No." I sit on the bed next to her. "But, Liam kissed me tonight. I guess he thought I was into him, but I think he thinks everyone is into him. I kind of freaked and he figured out that the pictures of you and me were real. He knows I'm a lesbian."

I can see the gears inside her head moving rapidly. "Is he going to tell anyone? If your parents figure out the truth, they'll make you leave Brunswick. They'll send you away."

"I know," I stammer, taking her hand again. "Liam and I reached an agreement. I wanted you to know before there are pictures."

I can tell she, understandably, doesn't like where this is headed. "What's he making you do?"

"I just have to pretend to be with him. His parents think he's calmed down with his playboy lifestyle, and you know I need to pretend to be straight. We're not going to kiss or anything. It's a show for our parents' sakes."

Nova sighs and her eyes flick up to the ceiling for a moment in frustration. "That's not fair."

"I know and I understand if you want to end things with me. I wish I could be open about us. Believe me, that's all I want in this world." I can feel the tears in my throat. "I know this is all probably more complicated than you wanted it to be. I know it's asking a lot to be with me."

"I can make that decision for myself," she says a little harshly. Then, she sighs. "I'm not going anywhere. I meant that it's not fair to you, like, mentally."

"Thank you for understanding. I think I'm okay, mentally speaking. I mean, I've faked it for this long. What's a little longer?"

I can tell she's still not happy with this idea and I know it's a lot of understanding on her end. I hope she knows how much this means to me. "Just talk to me, okay?" She's softened a little now. "Anything that happens or however you feel, I want to know. I worry about you."

I kiss her again. "I love you."

"I love you, too. Things will get easier, you know that, right?"

"That's what I keep telling myself," I admit. "I keep telling myself that once I'm eighteen, things will be better. Or, once high school is over, things will be better. I've got a countdown going in my head."

She pumps my hand. "You shouldn't have to live that way, you know? It sucks that you have to wish your life away. I want this time with you as memories, good ones."

I glance at our hands clasped on my lap. "Can we settle for some good, some not so good?"

"Sure," she smiles. "And when all this is over, I'm kicking Liam's ass for manipulating you."

17

It's Halloween night, a holiday my parents hate probably as much as they hate the devil himself. I never got to go trick or treating with my friends growing up, not even a church trunk or treat. For me, Halloween was always just another day, a day I'd spend looking out of my window watching the other kids in their costumes as they'd be hauling bags of candy from each house to the next. My parents would leave brochures on the porch in a bowl instead of candy, explaining why Halloween was 'the devil's holiday'. It only took a couple of years before word traveled that my house was full of 'bible thumpers' and our house was skipped altogether.

Brunswick doesn't condone the celebration of Halloween either, but we're all teenagers who don't do as we're told so multiple kids were given detention for wearing masks to school or wearing pieces of a costume over their regular uniforms today. One guy had a vampire cape over his uniform. Another girl was wearing goth makeup with an upside down cross on her forehead, which I'm pretty sure resulted in suspension. Even the mention of Halloween parties in our classes had been met with reprimanding, but that didn't stop anyone from talking about the party at Nate's house tonight. His parents don't care about Halloween, or it seems much of anything the way Nate talks about them. I've noticed that when he brings up his older brother he scowls a little, but I don't pry. Tonight's party is set to be the party to end all parties with Nate quickly climbing the social ladder set to surpass Liam on being the most sought after junior at Brunswick.

Liam steps through the front door of my house after

knocking politely dressed nicely in khaki slacks, a light blue dress shirt with the sleeves rolled to the elbow, and brown dress shoes. He looks like he's going to church, not a party. My parents are in the foyer to see us off. They think we're going out to dinner and a movie. Liam shakes Dad's hand, which is something my dad respects about Liam. The first time they'd met a couple of weeks after Liam and I broadcasted our relationship to the world, there hadn't been much conversation between my parents and Liam, not until Liam brought up that his dad worked in finance, which had been enough to break the ice between him and my dad. Liam had even made my dad laugh, but I don't remember what was said.

Since then, my parents have been bringing up Liam whenever they can, digging for any details of our relationship. I've had to come up with things I know they want to hear, like that Liam is well-liked by the teachers at our school and that he's involved with his church—all lies, of course. It's easy to pretend, especially when I replace Liam's name with Nova's in my head. My parents haven't brought up my sexuality since Liam has been in my life, which is a relief. I can tell they're relieved, too. Maybe they think Nova was a phase, but they've been treating me like they did before I came out. Every time Mom smiles at me or Dad gives me a look of acceptance I keep thinking it's going to make me feel better, but all I feel is distaste. None of it is real and I know if they knew the truth, they'd hate me again.

Liam and I don't talk much in the car on the way to Nate's house. We don't talk that much, anyway. We don't have anything in common except being each other's alibis. He's not a bad guy. Sometimes, he even makes me laugh. Most of the time, though, he's arrogant, and he's really good at finding ways to use people for his benefit. I don't blame him for that, though. From the little I know about his family, his parents only love each other in public and his older brother has had some issues with the law in the past. Liam has grown up around selfish people and aren't we all small reflections of the people around us?

The Wall of Nova

♀

Nate's Halloween party looks like every other teen party I've seen in movies except some people have shown up in costume and there are sparse decorations someone has half-assed and attached to the walls with clear packing tape. Since Liam has to take me home in a few hours, he's drinking now to sober up later, or so he says. I'm not drinking at all in case I have to find another way home. Liam and I have agreed that for tonight, we don't have to act like we're together since I'm sure he's going to sneak off with someone else and I'm not concerned with pretending. The longer Nova and I are together and the more time we spend together in my bed when she sneaks in through my window the less I'm starting to care about the agreement Liam and I made.

I elect to find Jill since she's not the party type either and I have no idea where Kallie is. I find Jill leaned against a wall in the living room, her eyes scanning the room behind her circle glasses that make her look like she's time traveled from the sixties. She grins at me as I lean next to her and follow her eyes around the room. There's a couple making out on the couch next to a small group smoking on the same couch. I can see Jill blush a little as she keeps shyly watching the couple.

"They're not very subtle," I joke. I have to talk a bit loud over the music, but she nods so I know she hears me.

I don't know much about Jill. We haven't had much of an opportunity to talk mostly because we're never around each other outside of the rest of the group. She doesn't talk much when we're around each other, anyway. She seems to watch people and I've noticed that her facial expression will change depending on what she sees like she's saying something in her head, but she either doesn't want to say it out loud or maybe she doesn't realize that what she's saying is staying inside her head.

She's watching me out of the corner of her eye and I realize she must have said something that I didn't hear. "Sorry, the music is loud. What did you say?"

She gets closer to me. "You don't kiss Liam." She's not asking a question or is even acting like she's curious about it. She's saying it like it's something she's noticed while people watching.

"I don't like PDA," I say quickly. "It's not my thing."

She seems to understand and her attention goes back to the room. The way she watches people, it's like she's memorizing details of each person in case she would have to pick them out of a police line up. I'll bet if I asked her later what any person in the room was wearing she could tell me down to the last detail of someone's necklace.

A while later, Kallie finds us and tells us that Nate wants a group to play a make-out game, probably because a game is the only way he's going to get someone who's not a freshman to willingly do anything with him. Our group, plus some random people I don't really know, huddles into a spare room with some bookshelves and a reading chair. Nate explains the rules of the game, which involve the small closet in the room and a timer on someone's phone.

As the game is played, people around me are paired off and spend some time in the closet while the rest of the group make dumb comments to the respective couple from outside. Jill is the only person in the room not playing, instead electing to sit in the reading chair with a random book in her lap, but I notice that she's watching us, anyway. I haven't been chosen to go into the closet and I'm starting to think I've been looked over, thankfully.

"Let's make things interesting," Nate slurs, drunk, to the rest of the group. He points to Kallie, who's already been in the closet twice. "You and…" He looks around the group, extending his "and." He points at me. "You." Before now, every couple in the closet has been a girl and a guy.

I glance at Liam, but he's whispering in some girls ear being no help. Kallie is my friend, but I think back to my first day at Brunswick when she offered to kiss me. She hasn't mentioned the night she drove me home from that bonfire party and I started to believe that I'd made up her disappointment in my head. I doubt she cares that Liam and I are 'together'. She's been acting like my best friend since then, still touching me more than she probably should. I stand slowly and Kallie grabs my hand before leading me to the closet, which barely fits us. I can hear the comments of Nate and some other guys outside the closet, including some suggestive whistles.

Kallie's hand goes to the light switch, which is currently flipped on. "On or off?" She's waiting on my answer. "It's no big deal," she says casually. "It's just a kiss."

I feel the panic rise in my chest and even if I wanted to kiss Kallie, which I don't, I remember Nova asking me before if I'd kissed Kallie and how scared she'd been that I was going to say yes. A casual kiss, or not, I wouldn't hurt Nova like that or keep something like that from her, not that I could with social media being a thing.

"Why should we give them the satisfaction?" I'm passing the time. "I mean, why do they deserve for us to kiss for their benefit? Isn't that really sexist?"

She thinks it over. "It is." Her hand leaves the light switch, leaving the light on. "Though, it could be fun. I know you've kissed a girl, but I haven't. I'm kind of curious."

I feel a blush go over my cheeks and I remember how casual Nova had been about her being my first kiss just to get it out of the way. Still, I'm with Nova now and maybe if the circumstances were different and I was single, maybe I'd allow Kallie to kiss me just so she'd know what it's like to kiss a girl, but kissing her would be wrong, even if it didn't mean anything.

"I don't know," I say defensively. "Kissing means a lot to me. It's a big deal for me to kiss someone."

She seems to understand what I'm saying. "Yeah, okay." Her eyes glance to the closet door. "We might want to pretend we did, though. They can't know you chickened out. They'll never let you live it down."

I glance at the door too. "What do you suggest?"

She pulls her lipstick from her pocket and lightly brushes it against my lips before smearing it a little at the edges. "There. Now they'll be none the wiser."

I smile. "Thank you."

"No big deal," she shrugs. "That's what besties are for. If you ever change your mind, I'm down."

In the time remaining, Kallie and I whisper a conversation trying not to laugh too loudly so no one figures out that we're not making out in the closet. There's a box of Nate's family photos that we go through, laughing at Nate's childhood haircut that looks like small spikes on top of his head—frosted tips and all, and a shark tooth necklace. His older brother, the one he seems to loathe, isn't in many photos that look a few years older. Nate's mom looks significantly older in recent photos.

I flip around one of the pictures of Nate and his family, one without his brother. "What's up with Nate's family?"

Kallie glances at the picture. "Liam knows more than I do, but I remember Nate was gone a lot last year. His mom got sick. Cancer, or something. Then, his brother, Paul, moved himself and his family back here to be around her. I don't think Paul was around a lot before she got sick, so Nate kind of hates him for that."

When we hear the timer go off on the phone outside, we pack the pictures away and step out of the closet together. Nate lets out a low whistle and he's looking at my lips. "You sure do have a habit of making out with girls," he laughs.

"You're the one who put us in there together," Kallie points out to him. "What did you think was going to happen?" She winks at him before sauntering back to the group.

Nate's hand brushes my arm. "Liam's a lucky guy finding a girl who will hook up with other girls. When's it going to be my turn?"

I want to feel bad for Nate because of his older brother abandoning him when he was younger, only to come back and be the golden child when their mom got sick. I want to feel bad because he almost lost his mom, and still could, depending on her current situation. But, it's hard to feel bad for someone who gives me every reason to think of him as a creep.

I take my arm away from his touch. "It won't." I don't wait for him to say anything, or for him to touch me again.

For the rest of the time I have left at the party, I stick around Kallie and Jill. Kallie does most of the talking, as usual, as she talks about different people at the party that I don't know. She seems to know everyone and even details about people that I wouldn't think she'd know because I've never seen her talk to any of these people. Jill seems to enjoy listening to Kallie talk, probably because she gets to piece people's stories together with the way they look.

When it's time for me to leave, I go to find Liam somewhere in the party. I've checked the main rooms downstairs, but he doesn't seem to be here anymore. I find Henry who's hanging out with some people I don't know in the kitchen where it's a little quieter. "Have you seen Liam?"

Henry takes a sip of his drink, his eyebrows raising like he has a secret. "You might want to give him a few minutes," he laughs.

The rest of the group attempts to hide their laughter too. I eye Henry. "I don't know what that means."

"It means Liam's currently between someone's legs at the moment, sweetie," one of the girls says. She thinks I'm stupid. Henry laughs again and I wonder if he was planning to keep my fake boyfriend's cheating from me a secret forever.

I think about finding Liam anyway to act like the girlfriend who just discovered her boyfriend cheating on her at a party, but then I decide that embarrassing both of us isn't a good idea. If I pretend I don't believe Henry and the girl he was with then I can pretend that Liam and I are still together. I knew he wasn't going to pretend to be with me tonight, but I thought he'd at least be careful. He could get into trouble with his parents if they find out he's back to being his usual self.

I go back to where Kallie and Jill are still in the spare

room with the bookshelves. "Are either of you sober enough to drive?"

Jill half raises her hand, sat in the chair. "I am. I don't drink."

Kallie is sat on the floor in front of her. She squeezes her eyebrows together. "Is everything okay, Casey?"

I nod, keeping up the facade. "I just have to get home and I can't find Liam."

Kallie and Jill exchange a look. "What do you mean you can't find him?" Kallie asks. She knows. They both do. Liam's reputation for being a cheat is still going strong.

"I just mean, he wasn't with Nate or Henry," I shrug. "He's probably drunk anyway, and he drove me here."

"SuperGirl," Jill says. "Bright blonde, freshly bleached. Brown eyes, one slightly bigger than the other. Freckles on her chest, but too much makeup to see the ones on her cheeks. She has on silver hoop earrings and rose-colored lipstick."

Kallie still has her eyebrows pulled together. "Who are you describing?"

Jill glances at me nervously. "The girl I saw Liam go upstairs with."

"Why didn't you say anything?" Kallie asks her.

Jill shrugs. "I didn't think anything of it."

Kallie stands from where she is on the floor. "Alright, let's go." She stumbles a little and I catch her elbow. She steadies herself, taking a breath. "He can't get away with this."

"It's not a big deal," I tell her. I look at Jill. "Can you take me home, please?"

Jill stands from the chair, but she waits on Kallie's permission before she gives me an answer. Kallie looks at me. "Your boyfriend is cheating on you and you don't want to throw him out of a window?"

"No, I don't," I tell her. "I want to go home."

Kallie looks at Jill, then back to me. "You don't seem that upset."

I know the clock is ticking closer to my curfew and I'm

already going to have to explain why Liam didn't drive me home. I don't need to be pushing the lie by being late. "I am," I lie. "But I can't freak out right now. I have a curfew and I can't break it."

"Okay," Kallie concedes. "Let's go."

The car is quiet except for the occasional navigation Kallie gives since she knows where I live. I know the directions to my house from both schools and from places Mom and I frequent, but Nate's house was on the other side of town, which isn't a place I'm familiar with. I half expect Kallie to keep asking questions, but she's only flipping through the radio stations and then watching out of the window when she finds a song she likes. I keep meeting Jill's eyes in the rearview mirror and I think she's expecting me to be crying or something. I'm not upset at Liam for hooking up with someone, though I am angry that he wasn't more subtle and now there's a chance this fake relationship is ruined. Once again, I don't feel like I've been given a choice about something that's happened in my life.

When Jill pulls down my street, I get her to pull over to the side where Nova used to. Kallie turns around in her seat to look at me. "Liam has been one of my best friends for years. He's always been a player and he's never really had a girlfriend. When he confirmed that you guys were together, I thought maybe he'd changed. I'm sorry he didn't."

I hate that Kallie feels guilty over something she shouldn't. It's not her fault that Liam is the way he is. I feel guilty that she believes that I'm hurt over Liam. I feel obligated as her bestie to tell her the truth in order for her to know that nothing Liam is doing or will do, is her fault. "I need to tell you both something, but it can't leave this car."

I didn't think the truth was going to come out so soon with them, but with Liam 'cheating' on me tonight and that weird moment in the closet earlier with Kallie, I know I owe them both an explanation. I can't have Kallie going home feeling guilty and Jill happens to be here too. I think I can trust her since she doesn't talk much.

Kallie and Jill exchange a look. "Did you sleep with him?" Kallie asks.

"No," I say defiantly. "Promise me."

"We promise," Jill says, then Kallie nods in agreement.

I only mean to tell them that the relationship between me and Liam is fake and why we've had to fake the relationship, but then as I'm talking I feel my chest swell at the thought of Nova and her name leaves my lips before I can stop myself. I tell Jill and Kallie everything: accidentally coming out, my relationship with Nova, Pride, and even about my parents and their threat to put me in conversion therapy if I screw up at Brunswick.

When I'm done, Kallie is the first to speak. "I'm not going to lie, that kind of makes me more offended that you refused to kiss me in the closet earlier." I can tell she's kidding.

Jill has turned around in her seat as I've told them everything. "Do you know that you chew your thumb a lot?"

I pull the side of my thumb from my mouth. "Nervous habit." I glance between them. "I need you both to keep my secret. If it comes out that I've been lying, I'm screwed."

It's not a confirmation from Jill that I need. Not only does she barely talk, but even when she does, not that many people listen. It's Kallie that I'm worried about not because I don't trust her, but because she talks a lot and there's a chance she could slip up. She's like Kaida in that way.

"Duh," Kallie says. "I don't want you going anywhere. You're, like, the coolest person, besides me, in our group. No offense, Jill."

"I know," Jill mumbles.

"I think it's cool you have a girlfriend," Kallie continues. "I mean, she's a little scary looking with her fashion sense and everything, but if that's your type, then that's your type."

"She's actually really sweet once you get to know her," I defend. "She's just very passionate. That's what I like about her." It feels nice to talk about my girlfriend with people who don't know her and who won't judge me.

"Nova," Kallie says like she's dissecting her name. "That's pretty. I'd like to meet her sometime."

I smile thinking about the half a second Nova seemed jealous of Kallie. "She thinks you're pretty," I tell Kallie for the ego boost.

I see a slight blush on Kallie's cheeks and I don't think it's the alcohol. "Everybody wants me." I can tell she's using her confidence to cover her embarrassment. "But, nobody can have me."

I see Jill roll her eyes and by the way her top lip quivers I know she's saying something in her head that she's probably not going to say out loud. I laugh at how ridiculous Kallie is being. "I don't think anyone could handle you."

This makes Kallie laugh too. "You're right."

I glance out of the car window. "I should go. Thank you both, for everything."

"What are you going to do about Liam?" Kallie asks. "No one else knows that he's your beard."

"Nothing," I shrug. "I'm going to pretend I don't know that he's with someone else tonight."

Kallie seems unsure. "Okay. We'll back you up on that." Jill nods, agreeing.

I feel a weight has lifted from my chest now that I've come out to Kallie and Jill. The first time I came out to my friends at MLK, it didn't feel like I had a choice and I didn't have a choice with my parents. Before that when I'd come out to my Arizona friends, I'd felt pressured because I had just turned 15 and I was convinced that if I didn't come out then that waiting would be too late and that no one would believe me. But, tonight, I had a choice. I wasn't forced or pressured to come out, but I did it because I wanted to. I didn't want to lie to them anymore or have them feeling bad for me over Liam. I don't know what I expected them to do, but I was still relieved that they not only accepted me but seemed happy for me.

My parents meet me in the foyer when I come through the door. I'm only a couple of minutes late. They're looking over my shoulder, surprised to see me alone. "Liam didn't feel well," I explain. "He needed to get home and lay down."

"Oh," Mom says. "Well, I hope Liam starts to feel better soon."

"I'm fine, though," I add, knowing she wasn't going to ask.

Dad eyes me. "Were you wearing lipstick when you left?"

I feel my blood go cold. I'd forgotten that Kallie had put her lipstick on me in the closet to convince the others in the group that we kissed. Not only that, but it's also a bit smeared. To what extent, I don't know.

My fingers go to my lips and I laugh nervously. "Yeah, I was," I lie. "I guess I forgot to touch it up after dinner." I smooth the edges of my lips.

"Looks nice," he says flatly. He turns to go down the hall. I've never been more thankful that my dad doesn't pay enough attention to notice my makeup or usual lack thereof.

"I appreciate a gentleman who gets you home on time," Mom says.

"He is that," I fake smile.

18

As the weeks pass, my life at home becomes easier. Easier, not easy. Dad remains himself and Mom remains the shell of whoever she was before I ever knew her. But, things are as normal as they've ever been. On Friday nights, I'm with my Brunswick friends at Luigi's, sometimes going to parties, but staying close with Kallie and Jill while we're there, separated from everyone else. Nova sneaks into my room after my parents are asleep as often as she can as often as we risk. It's not as much as I want, obviously. I want her with me every day and night, but I have to be smart about it. Every time she comes she has something to add to the wall in my closet, a sort of shrine to our relationship hidden from sight by my clothes. The wall is covered with pictures, drawings, and anything sentimental from the time we've spent together. One of the newest pieces is a small poster, like one from a CD booklet, of Penny, the lead singer of Nova's, and now my favorite band, Penny Loafers. It's not the prettiest shrine, but it's ours and I love it all the same.

    I'd never really had a 'boyfriend' before we moved here and despite my arguments, my parents insisted that Liam and his family come to our house for Thanksgiving, a holiday I'd listened to Nova rant about as I'd laid on her chest and listened to her lungs strain from her frustrations. She'd run her fingers through my hair as she talked, which I think was the only thing that kept her from lighting something on fire. When Liam's family came to my house for the 'colonizer holiday', as Nova had eloquently put it more than once, anyone watching from the outside would have thought that Liam and I had announced our engagement. Naturally, our dad's got on like old friends. Our mom's, on the other hand, couldn't have been more different, not that either of them mentioned this as to not kill the buzz. By the time they left that evening, my dad was smiling bigger than I'd ever seen him smile and my mom was pruning her fingers from scrubbing pans in order to get her frustrations out.

At school, people have been looking at me and Liam strangely and whispering about us when we pass them in the hallway. Nearly everyone knows that Liam 'cheated' on me at Nate's Halloween party, but it's this big secret everyone is keeping away from me and I learn that some people think I 'cheated' first with Kallie in the closet. Liam never fessed up to what he did and Nate and Henry must be some of the best 'bros' out there because I don't think either of them has told Liam what I know. It's not that I would expect him to be honest with me. Being honest was never part of the plan. If he were a decent fake boyfriend or even a decent human, he would tell me what happened and we could 'make up' in front of everyone, but it's not in his nature to take the blame for anything. Kallie seems to know this too because she drags me away from Liam as much as she can.

I'd spent the night at Kallie's house just after Thanksgiving, which apparently had convinced my parents without a shadow of a doubt that I was no longer interested in girls because Mom had been excited when I'd mentioned Kallie's invite. Kallie had picked me up from my house and based on my mom's reaction to Kallie, Kallie seems to be the daughter that my mom always wanted: poised, naturally beautiful, and seemingly interested in everything my mom says, even when she talks about boring stuff. I don't let that get to me mostly because I know the real Kallie and I know that Kallie is only pretending to be perfect for my sake. If my mom knew the real Kallie, she'd never want me around her again.

Kallie's parents are both lawyers, which was made obvious to me over dinner as they both were on their phones and occasionally leaving the table in the middle of conversations to speak with clients in the other room. When I'd brought up her parents' disinterest in her life, Kallie had shrugged, said that it was "no big deal", then quickly changed the subject away from her home life and back to my life, in particular, Nova. Kallie had wanted to know everything about her and about everything Nova and I had done in our relationship, including details that I hadn't been comfortable talking about, but managed to skim over enough to satisfy her curiosity.

When we went to bed that night, me sleeping on a blow-up mattress on the floor next to her bed, Kallie seemed upset by something and she'd had this look on her face like her stomach hurt. When I'd asked her what was wrong, she'd said "nothing" before turning the lights off and flipping on her white noise machine sat on the top of her desk, which I didn't find soothing because it reminded me of when I'd leave a VHS on too long as a kid and the TV would turn to an annoying static until I flipped the TV off.

I don't know what time it was, but at some point, Kallie was saying my name waking me from a deep sleep. She was leaning over her side of the bed waiting on me to wake up. I'd rubbed my eyes and again asked her what was wrong. In the dark, she still looked nervous and like she could be sick at any moment. I'd braced myself for her to puke, but she didn't. Instead, she'd sighed and for the first time, I saw her vulnerable.

"Can I tell you something?" Her voice was low and I could barely hear her.

"Anything," I'd whispered back, convinced she wasn't going to be sick anymore.

"I think I like girls, too," she'd said slowly, deliberately choosing her words.

There was a part of me, a big part, that had suspected that. Like Nova had told me the day I'd come out to her, I had to work on my gaydar, but with Kallie, I was almost certain I was right before she'd told me.

I'd sat up on the mattress then, smiling at her. "I'm glad you trust me enough to tell me that."

She'd smiled and she'd wiped her nose with the back of

her hand. I hadn't realized she'd been crying and I'd felt guilty that she'd probably been crying for a while before she woke me up. Then, she'd laughed and extended her other hand to me, the one that didn't have her snot on it, to hold.

"Nova's lucky," she'd said, laying down again with my hand in hers. She was silent for a while as I was still sat up, watching her. Then: "I wish I'd known you sooner."

Eventually, she fell asleep and I'd held her hand until she'd flipped over.

♀

I'm on winter break from Brunswick and for the first time in what seems like forever, Nova and I have a plan to see each other in public without the cover of darkness or behind a closed door. I've been on my parents' good side with 'dating' Liam and keeping my nose clean at Brunswick, so I decide to cash in on my good behavior card with Mom. She's been busy since the Sunday after Thanksgiving with the church readying events for Christmas, which is to my benefit since she hasn't been keeping her eyes too focused on me. If there's one thing I've learned from my mother, it's how to manipulate a situation so that the other person involved, my dad usually in her case, is none the wiser.

I go downstairs and find Mom nearly buried in empty shoe boxes and various other things she has to do for the church at the dining room table. I plaster on my best I'm still your little girl smile as I get her attention over one of the flat boxes she's folding. "Do you need some help?"

She continues to fold. "No, I've got it."

I linger in the dining room. "I was thinking since I'm not doing anything, I could take your list to town and grab everything you need."

She pauses in her folding and watches me for a moment. I don't drop my smile, trying to be as casual as I can be despite my insides begging her to let me go. Her eyes drop back down to the box and her head tilts to motion to the kitchen. "Bring me my purse."

I grab her purse from the kitchen counter and hand it to her. As she digs through it, I eye the red and green boxes on the table with the plane on the center. "Are these the ones that go to Africa?"

She brings out the list and sets the folded paper torn from a notebook on the table. "They are." She continues to dig and pulls out her car keys, then her wallet. She pushes the list and the car keys toward me. Then, she grabs some cash from her wallet and slides that over, too. "Don't be too long." She begins to pack her purse back up. "And I expect change. I've already priced those items, so I'll know."

I grab everything from the table and shove the list and money in my pocket, palming the keys. "Understood. See you in a bit."

Nova had offered for me to come to her place, but after we thought about it, we knew we'd have no privacy with her older brother, Jesse, being home, not to mention Nan and Pops who have good intentions, but tend to drag us into too-long conversations. Nova's car is already in the abandoned grocery store parking lot when I pull up in Mom's car. I hardly get my seatbelt off before she's standing outside my driver's side door.

She opens it the rest of the way and I laugh as she pulls me into her arms. "Hi," I whisper against her shoulder.

"Hi," she echoes against my lips as she kisses me.

She takes my hand and we go to her car. She's cleaned out the backseat, more likely given everything away, and we climb in. The car is still running and warm. We kiss for a while, Nova's music low in the background while we enjoy each other's company. She leans back against the door and I sit backward between her legs so she can hold me. She has her fingers interlocked with mine and she's breathing slowly against my hair.

"I wish I could love you openly," I say as I play with her fingers.

"One day," she says against my hair. "One day, we'll have our own place and we can be as open as we want to be. No one will be able to say we can't."

Ever since the first time she told me she loved me outside my house before I was made to come home, I've been picturing what a life with Nova would be like. I got a small taste of that when I'd stayed at her house, navigating the small bedroom and single bathroom. I'd imagined it would be like too in our studio apartment somewhere far from here, but close enough for us to visit Nan and Pops. Recently, I'd talked to Nova about our future and to my relief, she'd been thinking about it, too.

"I wish I didn't feel so guilty about you having to be back in the closet for me," I tell her.

"No one could put me back in," she laughs. "I'm just as out and loud as I've always been. I just have to whisper when I say your name."

Knowing I have limited time, Nova has agreed to help me with the list Mom gave me as long as I agree to let her treat me to a date since we haven't really had a proper one. Mom's list takes a short trip to the Christian book store in town for the church's version of White Elephant, plus a trip to the dollar store for the shoe boxes. That doesn't take long, so Nova and I have a couple of hours to do whatever we want.

I'd followed her to town in Mom's car, so I put the gifts in the trunk before Nova and I walk around town. When she takes my hand, I notice people eyeing us and I'm nervous that one of the strangers somehow knows my parents.

I pump Nova's hand once. "I don't want to get caught."

Her thumb rubs mine. "What's more important to you, living unapologetically and holding my hand in public, or hiding and letting your parents scare you?"

"My parents could still decide to send me to a conversion camp," I remind her.

After a few tense seconds of her eyes on mine, she drops my hand. "I know."

"I'm sorry," I say quickly. "It was different when I wasn't me at Pride."

She offers a tight-lipped smile. "I don't blame you."

The Wall of Nova

Even though we're not holding hands, I still walk close to her and sneak a touch here and there on the back of her arm, or graze my pinky on the side of her hand when I'm sure no one's going to notice us. She leads me to a second-hand record shop that has multiple dehumidifiers, but they don't completely mask the musky smell of the older records.

Nova quickly navigates modern records. "I thought it'd be fun to pick random records and listen to them together. Pops has a record player in the den."

"Do you think we'll have time before I have to go home?"

"Plenty," she smiles.

I look at the crates of multi-colored record sleeves. "How do we decide?"

"Close your eyes." I do so. She stands behind me and I feel her hands cover my eyes. "No cheating," she teases.

"I'm not," I laugh.

She laughs too. "Pick up a random one and we'll buy it."

I linger my hands over the crates and touch my fingertips to the tops. Since I can't see the records, I feel the edges for one that seems the newest. "This one," I say as I pull the record from the crate.

I open my eyes as Nova drops her hands and takes the record from me. "Good choice." She lays the record to the side. "My turn," she says as she closes her eyes and zombie steps with her hands out in front of her.

We go back and forth choosing random records. When we have a few between us, Nova buys them and we walk back through town to our respective cars. I follow her back to her house, which I haven't been back to since my parents made me move back home. I've thought of Nan and Pops often and I even thought about calling to check in, but I never got up the courage, mostly because I had no idea what I would say.

Nan greets us at the door, pulling me into a hug. Nova tries to explain that we have to keep to a schedule, but Nan insists on one cup of tea while she, Pops, and I catch up on what's going on in my life. As I'm telling them what's been going on at home, leaving my life at Brunswick mostly out of it, an older guy, I assume to be Jesse, walks into the kitchen wearing pajamas and his hair messed up as if he's just woken up.

"Jesse, this is Nova's girlfriend, Casey," Nan explains.

Jesse rubs his eye, yawning. "Hey," he says casually as he continues into the kitchen, barely glancing in my direction.

I hear Jesse going through the fridge, then reappearing with snacks and a soda in his hands. "Don't ruin your dinner," Nan warns.

"I won't," Jesse says as he rounds the corner.

Nova glances at the clock on the wall above the dining room table. "Okay, Nan, we don't have much longer."

Nan nods. "Go on, then. Let Pops know if you need help with that old player."

"It can be finicky," Pops agrees.

Nova takes me toward the side of the house opposite her room and the kitchen, a place I'd never really been when I'd stayed here. She slides open a door to a den with beautiful long windows and vaulted ceilings. The floors are wooden, but there's an old faded rug in the center. Nova goes to a table in the corner and brings the player to the middle of the rug, the cord barely reaching. It only takes her a couple of minutes to figure out the old player and soon she's putting on a record.

She lays back on the rug and stares up at the ceiling while the record plays in the room. I lay next to her with the player at our heads, holding her hand as we listen to the music play. We make occasional comments about our choices and Nova switches the records out after a few songs each. We decide we really only liked one of the records and she tears off the coolest artwork from the, ironically, worst record for me to tack to our wall.

19

It's the weekend before Christmas and our town is putting on a Christmas/winter festival. At Brunswick and at my house, it was referred to as a Christmas Festival as if pairing the festival with a season as to not exclude those that don't celebrate Christmas was somehow spitting in God Himself's face. The kids at my parent's church (and by association my church) are putting on a play at the festival, so if I wasn't already invited to hang out with Liam, Kallie, and the rest of the group, I'd have to go anyway. Mom has been put in charge of getting the play together and Dad had helped build the set, so they're both going to be preoccupied with that while the festival is going on.

We'd have festivals like this in Arizona, but it's different here. For one, it's actually cold, even though the locals have been complaining since Halloween that the weather shouldn't be warm enough to send their kids out in t-shirts. Secondly, Santa is riding around the festival in a convertible muscle car, not a police car or a fire engine like I'm used to. Every year, I've heard my parents complain that Santa was made more important than God at Christmas, but I never complained. I still got three presents because as my parents put it, "Three presents were good enough for the Son of God." Another thing that's different, and probably the weirdest thing, is the amount of fried food. Our festivals had fried food trucks, but here, it's taken to a new level. Basically, if it can be battered and fit in a deep-fry basket, it's going up on their hand-drawn menu.

My Brunswick friends and I are walking around the festival, Kallie with her arm looped through mine as she always does when we walk close to each other, and Liam's hand in my other since his parents are here too. Kallie hasn't mentioned the night I'd stayed at her place and what she told me, but she seems more comfortable around me now, not that she has ever known boundaries with me. My friends and I have filled our stomachs with food and hot chocolate and we've made it to the part of the festival with the games. Up ahead, I recognize a familiar nearly bald head sat in his chair while holding a water gun, aiming at the targets. Next to Lars, J.J has a cigarette dangling between their lips.

I release Liam's hand and I'm getting ready to invite him to meet my MLK friends when he takes my letting his hand go as an invitation to leave. He, Nate, and Henry break off from the rest of us to some other games. Kallie raises her eyebrows at me, noticing that sudden departure, too. She continues to hold my arm as Jill joins us in walking the direction we were initially headed.

"I think your aim is a bit off," I say to Lars, teasing him.

He glances over his shoulder at the same time J.J whips around to see who made the comment. They laugh, relieved. "Oh." They look from me to Kallie and Jill. "Brunswick kids?"

Kallie slides her hip out. "And what of it?" She's not actually annoyed, but she likes everyone to think she's being cute.

J.J shrugs, taking the cigarette from their mouth. "Nothing." They look back at me. "Kaida and Nova are around here somewhere."

"We'll go find them," I say. Lars has already gone back to target practice. I wave to J.J. "It was good seeing you."

"Yeah," they say, putting the cigarette back in their mouth and turning back to watch Lars.

As we walk to find Nova and Kaida, Kallie scoffs. "He's kind of a jerk."

"'They'", I correct. "And they're not so bad. They're protective."

Kallie eyes me. "Well, I don't think they like me very much."

"Was the person in the wheelchair their boyfriend?" Jill

asks.

"Lars," I inform. "And, yeah, J.J and Lars have been together for a while." I don't remember J.J touching Lars. "How'd you know?"

Jill shrugs. "When Kallie got cute with J.J, I saw Lars's shoulders tense a little."

"Figures," Kallie huffs. She momentarily puts her chin on my shoulder. "All the cute ones are taken," she pouts.

Kaida and Nova are standing by a photo booth, Nova propped up on a half wall and Kaida standing next to her, arms crossed. I can't keep my eyes off Nova as she smiles, laughing at something Kaida has said. I notice Nova's eyes skate over to me and the smile falters the slightest bit when her eyes to go Kallie's arm looped through mine. Kaida notices this too and the look on her face reminds me of the time she saw me at Luigi's my first Friday night at Brunswick.

"Hey," I smile at Nova. "I didn't know you were going to be here."

"We had nothing better to do," Kaida jumps in, protectively. She eyes Kallie. "You can't keep your hands to yourself, can you?"

Kallie flicks her eyes to me, confused by the hostility. Her arm drops from mine and she eyes Kaida. "I remember you. You're the girl who enjoys looking like a glow stick." Kallie smiles her charming hundred-watt smile. "I'm Kallie if you didn't already know." Her eyes flick back to me. "And Casey and I are besties, so I'm allowed to touch her."

Kaida's eyes flick to me as if she's waiting on me to say something. When I don't, her eyes go back to Kallie. "Do you even know Casey?" Kaida asks.

Kallie laughs. "I know she's gay if that's what you're asking." Her eyes go to Nova. "You must be Nova. I've wanted to meet you forever."

Nova pushes herself off the wall and gets between Kaida and Kallie. "It's nice to meet you, Kallie," she says sincerely. "Casey has told me a lot about you." This makes Kallie smile.

Nova's attention goes to Jill. "Are you Jill?" Jill nods. "Nice to meet you, too," Nova smiles.

Kallie flicks her eyes to me. "I see why you chose her."

I blush, a little embarrassed. I don't think Kallie likes me the way she'd said she did at her house, or maybe I'm hoping she doesn't because I don't want to hurt her. Either way, I don't want there to be a fight between Kallie and Nova because I'd choose Nova and I think they both know that. Nova and Kallie reach for my wrist at the same time. I barely noticed my hand by my mouth. Kallie stops at the last minute and Nova takes my hand, lowering it from my mouth.

Kallie laughs. "Sorry," she tells Nova. "I'm used to doing that at school."

Nova flicks her eyes between me and Kallie. "Yeah, good. At least someone is taking care of her over there." Nova drops my hand, suddenly nervous.

There's this awkward air between everyone and one look at Nova tells she's thinking the same thing that I am. She wishes it was just us here so that we could be together how we were the last time we saw each other. Our date had been perfect even if the records we chose weren't. Just laying on that old rug with her not caring about getting back home, or caring about much of anything, was the first time in a long time that I felt like I could take a breath even if it was just for a moment. Every time the song changed, I knew time was ticking by, but it felt like time was standing still for us. I found myself wishing that time would stop altogether, just to freeze for an eternity with only two things moving in the world: the needle on the record player and our chests with each breath.

Now, time is moving quickly and as the crowd starts moving toward the stage for the play my mom is putting on with the church kids, I know that my time with Nova is coming to a screeching halt for the time being. If I'd known she was coming, I would've prepared myself for this meeting of worlds. It feels like my old life, a life I'd thought was going to be my new life, and my new life are coming together, bur not mixing as well as I'd hoped.

I motion toward the stage, keeping my eyes on Nova. "My mom put the play together, so I have to be in the audience. Do you want to come?"

Nova's eyes flick over my head toward the stage and then to Kaida. "I don't think so," she says to me. "I shouldn't be too close." I'm pretty sure everyone present knows why she doesn't want to be close to where my parents are and to what extent of the consequences that would happen if Nova and I were spotted together.

"Right," I say casually. "I understand." I flick my eyes to Kallie before I look at Nova again. "Maybe after the show we can hang out?"

Nova has suddenly become uncomfortable and I can tell she's regretting coming to this festival tonight. "I don't think so," she says apologetically.

"We have somewhere to be, anyway," Kaida says pointedly to Kallie. Kaida looks at me. "There's a show tonight."

I try to not be offended that I wasn't invited, but if there have been other shows since the last one I went to with Nova, I haven't known about it. In fact, the group texts I used to be a part of have gone radio silent.

I invite Kallie to loop her arm through mine again and she does. I flick my eyes between Kaida and Nova. "Have fun," I try to say genuinely, but I think comes off cold.

Nova catches my eye and I can tell there's something she wants to say, but she doesn't. Kallie tugs on Jill's sleeve and the three of us turn as a single unit and head for the stage where the play has started.

20

This year, given how I've been on the straight (pun intended) and narrow since being at Brunswick, I half expected to wake up on Christmas morning to a car sitting in the driveway. Dad had talked about me having my own car once we moved here because he was going to be making more money at his new job. I wasn't expecting a new one or even a nice one, but something with four wheels and a motor would've suited me fine. Instead, when I wake up on Christmas morning, there's not a single gift beneath our tree. Now, I'm not some kind of spoiled brat who expects a million gifts or even three, but zero isn't what I was expecting at all.

I round the corner to the dining room in my pajamas where Dad is already sat at the table and Mom has a pot of oatmeal in hand, spooning some into Dad's bowl. Mom glances up long enough to see me, then goes back to serving Dad. Dad sips his coffee but doesn't seem to notice that I've come into the room. If I was another kid, one who had a much different life, I'd think my parents were faking me out. I'd think that there are gifts hidden somewhere in the house for a surprise. Or, maybe, Dad's going to lift his folded paper to reveal a car key with the car being kept at a secret location for the sake of a surprise. But, I didn't have that kind of childhood and I don't have those parents, so I know this is all for real. There's nothing special about this morning on the gift front.

I slide into my normal seat where there's an empty bowl on my placemat and a glass half filled with orange juice. "Merry Christmas," I mumble to my parents, attempting to keep the disappointment out of my voice.

The Wall of Nova

Mom stands next to me and spoons some oatmeal into my bowl. "Merry Christmas," she says with equal enthusiasm. She goes to her own seat and begins to sit down, then Dad sits his coffee cup down with a thud indicating its emptiness. Mom takes his cup and heads to the kitchen to refill it.

Dad eyes me with his hands held in front of him waiting on Mom to get back so we can do our morning prayer, which will be slightly different this morning given the holiday. "Are you seeing Liam today?"

Mom comes back with Dad's coffee and sits it down in front of him before going to her seat. "His family is out of town for Christmas," I tell him. "They're visiting his grandparents in Ohio." I'd asked Liam about Christmas at the festival, for appearance sake, and I was relieved when he told me he'd be away. He seemed relieved too and I'm sure he's going to find some trouble to get into up there.

Dad frowns slightly but doesn't make a comment. It's not like he and Liam are best friends or anything, but I think he would've been relieved to have anyone here that wasn't me or Mom. He extends his hands to me and Mom, and Mom and I lower our heads as Dad speaks in circles in his Christmas prayer. It goes on for what seems like forever and the smell of the oatmeal beneath my nose is torture on my empty stomach. Finally, he ends with an enthusiastic "amen", and Mom and I echo him with less enthusiasm.

It's hours later and today has been officially the weirdest and most boring Christmas I've ever had with my family. There were no hidden gifts, not that I'd really expected that to be the case. Mom spent most of the day in her bedroom and Dad spent the day in the living room in front of the TV. I wouldn't have even known it was Christmas if it wasn't for the fact that I had to call my grandparents back in Arizona who have no idea about how my life has been out here. My parents have conveniently not told them anything about me, which is, admittedly, for the best since the apples (being my parents) didn't fall far from their trees (being both sets of grandparents). For the sake of keeping my family stitched together, I'd mentioned Liam, which had me feeling like a big fat liar as I'd done so.

♀

Nova drops by once my parents have been asleep for a couple of hours. We haven't talked much since the festival, mostly because I didn't know what to say. Still, we've had this night scheduled since I got away with meeting her in secret while running errands for my mom and I knew Nova and I needed to talk, anyway.

I close the window quietly behind her and I notice she has a wrapped gift in her hands. "I thought you didn't celebrate Christmas."

She juts the gift out toward me. "It's not a Christmas gift. It's an apology gift for the other night. I'm sorry things were weird. I was jealous that Kallie was allowed to touch you at the risk of being seen, but I wasn't and haven't been since the beginning." She sighs. "I'm over that now and I understand, so I'm sorry."

After I'd gone home from the festival the other night, I was a little annoyed at Nova, and my MLK friends for being so standoffish to my Brunswick friends. I hadn't expected J.J or Lars to pay me much attention because they didn't much before, but Kaida being aggressive toward Kallie had surprised me. That night, I thought things might be over between me and Nova, especially since I hadn't heard from her since she, and the rest of the group, had left. I'd only stopped panicking when she'd replied to my goodnight text, echoing it. Even then, I wasn't sure, but her being here now, like this, must mean that we're okay.

I take the gift from her and sit at my desk chair. "I didn't think about the whole touching thing. I'm sorry." I nod to the gift in my hand. "You didn't have to get me anything. What happened the other night was on me, too." I open my desk drawer and pull out a gift I'd gotten Nova while she wasn't looking the day we'd hung out in town. "I'm sorry it's not wrapped." I hand her the gift, a pack of professional markers like the ones people use for comic books. "I wasn't sure if you'd like them."

She eyes the markers in her hands, smiling. "They're perfect." I move her gift to my desk as she wraps her arms around my shoulders. She gives me cheek kisses in quick succession. "I was scared that night," she says, releasing me. "I thought you'd dump me."

I take her hand. "I was scared you'd dump me," I smile nervously.

"Never," she smiles.

I grab her gift from my desk and unwrap the brown paper as quietly as I can. There's a plain rectangle box beneath the paper. I open it and pull out a glass oval statue with a flat bottom. Inside the glass are bubbles and a jellyfish that looks real, but I know it's been made out of glass, all one solid piece. It's heavy and I set it on my desk beneath the light of my desk lamp, which makes the pink jellyfish look even more real.

Nova catches my eye. "Do you remember when we first started talking and you kept sending me all of those ocean facts?"

I smile, remembering being at MLK with Nova. It seems like forever ago that she would pick me up at our spot and drop me off there after school every day. It seems like forever ago that I would be distracted by her flicking her tongue across her lip ring or how her hand would play with my hair band on her wrist, which she has yet to remove like it's become a part of her skin.

I sit her on my lap and wrap my arms around her. "I remember," I say against her bare arm since she's come out without a coat. "I wanted you to think I was cool."

She gives me a look. "And you thought that was the way to do it?" She brushes my hair with her fingers. "It's a good thing you're pretty and a good kisser because you're definitely not cool."

I squint my eyes at her. "Punk."

She touches her nose to mine. "Nerd." She kisses me.

21

I'm standing outside of Brunswick waiting on my mom to pick me up. We've been back in school from Winter Break for about three weeks and it's still cold out. From what I've been told, February is the coldest month in North Carolina and the month we're all most likely going to miss school due to snow and ice. Because I'm forced to wear a dumb uniform, my legs are freezing through my thin tights and the cardigan that's a part of the uniform on cold days is equally as thin. I pull the cardigan tighter around me as I wait, turning my head side to side searching for my mom's car. My friends, along with most everyone else, are already gone.

As time ticks by, campus attendance dwindles and once I see teachers begin to leave, I start to worry. I begin to imagine the terrible things that could've happened, then realize that I'm probably overreacting. She might have fallen asleep and her nap is going on longer than she intended it to. I call the home phone, but she doesn't answer. I text her cell phone and wait, but again, nothing. I call a few more times, flipping between calling the home phone and cell phone before I give up and figure I need another way home.

After thinking about it and weighing my options, I call Liam. He picks up on the last ring before it goes to voicemail. I explain why I'm calling him and after a few seconds of him thinking it over, he huffs and agrees to drive me home. The car ride with him is a little awkward since while he was gone over break, his parents caught him hooking up with some girl, so he was forced to 'apologize' to me over dinner at his place right before we came back to school. That had been awkward enough, but then his mom had sat me down and talked about how, as women, we have to deal with the things men do and learn to forgive because they have 'needs' we can't keep up with. I'd never been more thankful that mine and Liam's relationship was not only fake but that I'm a lesbian.

 Liam drops me off in my driveway and I quickly walk up to the house and through the front door. I can hear noises upstairs, like furniture being moved and heavy footsteps. I almost think we're being robbed, but I know my mom's movements when she gets overwhelmed. Her footsteps become clumsy like her brain is moving faster than her feet. I go upstairs and Mom is in my bedroom flipping my room upside down.

 My closet is bare and everything inside, including mine and Nova's things, are on the floor torn from the wall. I feel a chill go through my blood. "What are you doing?"

 Mom jerks her head toward me where she's been looking beneath my mattress. "How did you get home?"

 "Liam drove me. Why are you tearing my room apart?"

 She motions to the closet. "You lied to me."

 I stand in shock as I inspect the damage closer. Everything from the wall is torn and scattered across the carpet. The poster of Penny is ripped in half and each item from the wall has been shredded like confetti. "You fucked it all up," I sob, feeling sick to my stomach.

 My cussing has made her eyes widen. "Your father is on his way home." She's suddenly calm. She stands from the floor and inspects the mess with emotionless eyes. "You've had every chance in the world to do the right thing, but I'm done. You have a bed ready at camp. Start packing." As she walks by me, she extends her hand. "Phone," she orders.

 She shuts my bedroom door behind her as she leaves and I sink down to my knees on the floor, the pieces of paper on the floor bending against my knees and sticking to my tights. I sift through the pieces as I cry, attempting to piece them together like a jigsaw puzzle. It seems like every piece I grab doesn't fit anywhere and eventually, I sit back and stare at the mess on my floor, the carpet beginning to absorb the small pieces. I bite the side of my thumb until it bleeds and then I peel thin strips of skin away, keeping my screams trapped in my chest.

♀

I'm in the back of my dad's car with my bag at my feet on the way to the conversion camp. He'd come home early just as Mom had asked. I'd eventually picked myself up off of my bedroom floor and changed into normal clothes despite wanting to crumble to pieces like what's left of what had been on my closet wall. I'd slowly packed my things as I was contemplating climbing through my window and disappearing, but for some reason, I couldn't force my body through the window. All I could do was step on the pieces from my closet wall and push them further into the carpet until they were wrinkled beyond saving. I'd been sitting on the edge of my bed with my bag next to me as I waited for my dad to get home. I'd held Nova's gift in my hand, inspecting the jellyfish, feeling myself trapped in the glass with it. Just as I'd heard my dad walk into the house, angry that I'd caused him to miss another meeting, I tucked Nova's gift away in my bag in the front pocket of one of my hoodies to hide it, to have Nova with me.

Mom's in the passenger seat and the inside of the car is completely quiet, like how a bomb is quiet. My heart is thudding in my chest and my bloody thumb is back in my mouth, my teeth grazing the small wounds to keep my mind from wandering. My tongue flicks against the raw flesh and the taste of blood makes me feel queasy, but I can't stop. All I can imagine is my dead body swinging from the rafters of one of the cabins, like the boy from my old church. I imagine my body being found, my parents not caring that I was dead, and my death being used on either side of the narrative. People like my parents will say I killed myself because I couldn't cope with the guilt of being gay. The others, the ones like me, would know why I did it. The most I could hope for would be to be used as an example for other parents, for them to love their kids so their kids don't end up like me.

I quickly realize that I can't go through with 'therapy'. I'd rather die. I've never felt suicidal in my life, but the closer we get to the camp, and the further I get away from Nova, the more solid my choice has become in my brain. I'll miss Nova and I'll miss my friends. I hope Nova can forgive me. I hope she can find someone who loves her like she deserves to be loved. I hope she remembers me like how she saw me on Christmas, or how we'd been beneath the blanket fort in her bedroom the first time we kissed. I hope those are the memories she has of me, not the memory of what my body is going to look like inside my casket. I wonder how much makeup they'll need to cover my blue face or if my skin will look weird around my bulged eyes. My parents would probably decide on a closed casket to hide their shame.

A switch goes off in my brain, the kind that jolts my brain into realizing the obvious, and I know dying isn't an option. I have plans for my future, plans I've made with Nova. I can't give up on myself, or on us. I can't put her through my death. I can't allow her to feel any amount of guilt. I can't risk that she would hate me, even though I know she wouldn't. If I killed myself, I don't know if she would forgive me and the thought of being without her makes my chest ache. Whatever happens, I have to get to her, to get away from this life. The path my parents have laid out for me only has one end and I refuse to be a statistic. I feel myself starting to panic, my legs feeling like there are spiders inside. I have to go. I have to get out.

At the next stoplight, seconds away from turning green again, I grab my bag from the floorboard, knowing that it's now or never. I bolt from the backseat of the car, feeling the icy air hit my throat immediately. I run as fast as my legs will carry me across the road, narrowly avoiding other cars that are honking at me. My lungs are burning and my body is begging me to stop, but my brain is screaming at me to keep going. I cross multiple parking lots until my legs start to buckle beneath me and I know I have to stop before I pass out. I find an alley to hide in where I catch my breath behind a dumpster, which keeps me hidden from the road.

As I sit back against the brick wall, my bag on the ground next to me, my head begins to feel dizzy. Reality begins to kick in and I realize the choice I've just made. I can't go back to my life before, back to town, or anywhere close. I've made the choice to stay away and I don't know what happens now. I had to run. I should've run a long time ago when Nova told me to back in her room when my mom threatened to call the cops if I didn't come home. This was, of course, after my parents kicked me out in the first place. I should've called their bluff back then. I should've never gone back home and taken my chances if it meant being with Nova longer.

Now, I'm like Penny of the Penny Loafers, on my own at 16. I'd laughed when Nova had told me Penny's story. I'd thought it was ridiculous that she'd run away from home and that she managed to make it out in the world at such a young age. I never thought I'd be forced to do the same. I'd thought I was going to have some semblance of a normal high school career, or what was left of it. Kallie and I had talked about junior prom. We'd talked summer plans of her parents' lake house, too. Nova and I had talked concert season starting back and all the impossible ways we were going to follow one of the bands around the surrounding states, like groupies. Now, the uncertainty of everything is weighing on me and I don't know what to do.

I barely have any cash in my wallet, only a week or so worth of clothes, and I don't have my phone anymore since Mom took it from me. It's cold out and the nights are even colder, but I'd rather sleep on the streets and eat from dumpsters for the rest of my life than go back. I look around where I am and there are banners against the brick, advertisements for different beer brands. I don't know much about bars, but I know they have phones and I need to make a very important phone call.

After some weird looks from the patrons, the bar being

fairly full for it being just before five o'clock, the bartender allows me to use the bar's phone. It's a cordless phone, thankfully, and I take the phone, along with the bag strapped to my back, around the corner out of sight. Nova answers on the second ring. "Casey?"

"How'd you know?" I breathe. My lungs still hurt from running and I'm desperate for some water.

"Your cell is off." She sighs. "Where are you?"

I look around the bar. "I'm not sure. I think an hour or so from town."

"What do you mean? Why?"

I explain everything that happened this afternoon with my mom tearing my room apart and how I'd run from the car once we were stopped at a red light. It doesn't sound as cool and daring saying it out loud.

"Shit," she says when I'm done. "I knew something bad had happened when my call went straight to voicemail. How'd they know about us? I thought we were careful."

"Mom found the wall," I say casually.

I can hear Nova moving around. "Find out the street you're on. I'll come find you."

I think about Nova driving out here and picking me up. I wouldn't be able to go back with her, so she'd have to stay with me. As much as I like the idea of having her with me, I can't take her away from Nan and Pops. She's all they have with Jesse being away at college. I can't take her away from her friends either, or her whole life. I could never ask her to sleep on the streets with me, not when she has a warm bed and a loving family back home.

"Nova," I plead. "I can't come back home. My parents would never allow it. They'd find me and then…" I sigh. "I need to stay away for a while, maybe forever."

There's a beat of silence and I think she's hung up. "What the hell are you talking about? You can't be alone on the streets. It's not safe. Let me at least bring you some money. I can stay for a few days, you know, in a motel, or something. Nan and Pops would understand."

    I think it over, but just as I think about accepting her offer, I remember that I'm not far from where I jumped from the car. If my parents are looking for me, or have the cops looking for me, it won't take them long to find me if I stay in one spot. I have to keep running despite my body saying the opposite.

    "Thank you, but I need to keep moving," I tell her. "I'll call you when I can. I love you."

    "Casey." I hang up before she can change my mind.

22

    Spring has come to this small North Carolina town nestled between the mountains of North Carolina and the border of South Carolina. I've spent the last four and a half months working at a roadside diner here, a couple of hours away from home. I'd used the last bit of cash I had to buy a bus ticket and some food from the bus station vending machine, enough to survive until I found the job. I stayed at a shelter for the first three days I was on my own in this little town, but then, by day three, I was scared to stay since I'd woken up with a strange man standing over my bed, watching me. I had been weighing my options at work, which I'd started the day I decided to leave the shelter, when my manager at the diner, a middle-aged black woman who's blind in one eye and has barely any teeth left in her head named Ruby, found out I was homeless. She insisted I crash on her couch until I was up on my feet. Turns out, working at a diner that mostly sees truckers who don't tip well meant staying longer than I'd hoped, not that she seemed to mind. Over the time I spent with Ruby, we'd become close and she'd cared for me the way I'd always wanted my mom to care. She never let me go hungry or allowed me to pay for anything. I'd learned of her life, a single mother to a child in prison and she'd learned of mine, a child not accepted and waiting to reunite with the girl she loves.

    Now that I've been able to buy a car, an old one that's not in the best shape, but four wheels and an engine nonetheless, I know it's time to move on. It's time for me to get my life on track, even if I don't completely have the 'track' part figured out. Ruby has accepted my choice, and even though I'll miss her, we both knew our living situation wouldn't last forever. Ruby being her self, she's sent me on my way with Tupperware containers filled with the foods she insists stick to the ribs and that keep the blood warm. She also insisted that I take money from her even though I have some of my own. I've had to lie to her, a little, to keep her from feeling obligated to keep me any longer. She thinks I'm going back toward home and I've allowed her to think that for her sake. I wish I could go home, but that's not an option, not anymore. I turned seventeen a few weeks back, but only Nova knew that.

I've called her as much as I can over the past four months, keeping that tether to her. She's meeting me out here today before I leave. I want her with me, always, but I also know that taking her away from everything is selfish of me. If I'm meant to move on without her, a likely scenario, I at least wanted to say goodbye in person. I want to take the time to give her my heart, to allow her to take it back home with her. During those first few phone calls with Nova, I learned my parents never called the police to search for me. It's like they stopped caring, not even mentioning me in the community. My friends and Nova's grandparents, however, have been asking Nova about me. I've called Kallie a few times since I've been gone and I think she misses me as much as Nova does. Kallie told me she was seeing someone, a girl, and she thanked me in her own way for not being the first girl she kissed so she could have that first kiss with this girl. I'd told her I wanted to see her again, soon. She'd said "of course you do", then laughed her usual attention-grabbing laugh.

After checking that I have the few things I own, including my not-Christmas gift from Nova, which I'd slept with at the shelter to use for a weapon, I drive to the park in town where Nova and I have planned to meet. I find her on a grassy spot with a thin blanket beneath her. I thought she might look a little different, but she looks the same. When she smiles at me, her lip ring resting between her top front teeth, I can feel my heart leap into my throat trying to reach out to her, to be held by her.

I didn't realize how much I missed her and how a voice hadn't been enough all this time. There's this tinge of guilt that I hadn't allowed her to be with me these past four months. Then, there's the guilt that this could be the last time we have together and I already don't want to leave.

I sit down next to her and our hands immediately gravitate towards each other, the most natural thing in the world. I never stopped loving her even though distance and my situation should've wedged us apart. There was never a moment in these last four months that I thought about letting her go. It was thinking about her that kept me strong and kept me from giving up. She's, ironically, what kept me from home and running back to my parents. I knew I couldn't allow them to win, to put me in a place that would take me further away from Nova. Feeling her hand in mine, and the warmth of her skin against where my skin is cool from my car's air conditioning, I know that leaving is going to feel like I've lost one of my limbs. It's going to be the hardest thing I've ever done.

After we eat some of the food Ruby packed for me, and catch up on what we've been doing in our respective lives, Nova and I sit in silence for a while, enjoying each other's company. It's warm out, but that doesn't stop me from being held by her, to want to be as close as possible. I want to take her presence with me, the memory of her arm around me and the way her skin smells in the sun. I've always liked Nova like this the most, I think. She's loud and in your face, and she's unapologetic about who she is and what she believes in, but God when she's like this, soft, and the only sound she's making is the breath that escapes from between her lips, that's when I know my heart is hers, no matter what happens in the future.

"So, you did it," she says. I've just tucked my hair behind my ear and I can tell she's looking at me by the way her chin is tilted.

My hand goes to the top of my ear where I'd gotten it pierced after studying a picture of Penny I'd found online of her when she was 16. She'd also had her nostril pierced, but I'm not ready for that kind of commitment.

"We made a deal," I remind her. "If I got something pierced, you'd wear one of my blouses."

She laughs. "I didn't forget." She's silent for a beat. "I guess it's a good thing I'm coming with you, then."

I sit up, thinking I made her say that in my head. "What?"

She brings my hand to her lips and kisses the back of my hand. "My things are in the back of my car. Wherever you go, I go."

My other thumb goes to my mouth. "I don't know where I'm going yet," I tell her.

She takes my hand from my mouth and holds both of my hands in hers. She's still wearing my hair tie around her wrist, though it's nearly string and frayed elastic now. "I've been making a plan for us since the day you hung up on me after you'd escaped your parents. I have friends in Atlanta who have offered us a room. As long as we pay rent, it's ours."

"What about Nan and Pops? What about your life back home?"

"Nan and Pops knew as soon as I told them what happened to you that I wasn't going to stay long knowing you were out here. I made a deal with them that I'd finish out the school year, and thankfully, you stayed put that long." She smiles. "Everyone in my life knew that I'd follow you eventually."

I'm running out of reasons for her to go back and she knows that. "What about your future? If you drop out, that's it."

"That's not true," she assures me. I think she knew I'd pull out any excuse to not ruin her life, but she's prepared. "You can go pretty far with a GED nowadays. You can still be a Marine Biologist and I can have a successful zine that features my art. Plus, I don't want a future if you're not in it. We made a pact, remember?"

It was after the impromptu show the afternoon my parents kicked me out of the house. Nova and I had been sitting in her car cooling down after the show and we'd considered leaving with the clothes on our backs. This was before she'd kissed me, or that I knew I loved her. Even then, she was willing to run, like she never needed me to be the reason. I think Nova has that runner in her despite loving her life and loving her grandparents. It's like, even though she never knew her mom, that need to run is in her blood.

"I remember," I exhale. "I'm surprised you even waited on me to be the first one to run. I'd thought for sure you'd be the one to call me from a random phone and tell me you were gone, maybe never to come back."

"I thought the same thing." She pumps my hand, reassuring me. "We can have that future we talked about, Casey."

I lean my head against hers. "Do you think we can ever come back?"

She takes a few seconds to think. "It's not forever," she finally says. "Our friends can always visit us." She kisses my shoulder. "I love you and I know we can make this work. We can even get that cat you wanted."

"As long as I get my cat," I smile.

She sits up and starts to stand. "If we leave now, we can make a show." She extends her hand to me once she's stood.

I look at her hand, knowing if I take it, I've sealed our future. "Didn't you tell me once that stories about lesbians always end tragically?"

She wiggles her fingers. "Their stories aren't ours."

I take her hand. "No, they're not."

The End